THE

Heir

PART ONE

GEMMA WEIR

ST. AUGUSTUS PREPARATORY SCHOOL

VOS AUTEM ESTIS, QUI EST

EST 1917

The Heir - Part One
The Kings & Queens of St Augustus Series #3
Copyright © 2020 Gemma Weir
Published by Hudson Indie Ink
www.hudsonindieink.com

Cover design by Pink Elephant Designs
Interior design by Rebel Ink Co

The Heir- Part One/Gemma Weir – 1st ed.
ISBN-13 - 978-1-913904-30-2

Because villains need to tell their stories too.

THREE AND A HALF YEARS AGO

"Mr. and Mrs. Archibald, Miss Carrigan, please come in," the lawyer says, his greying hair styled into a combover that does nothing to disguise his bald head beneath.

Standing and following behind my parents I glance back at the waiting area and my sister, who is sitting playing games on her cell phone, and wish that I could stay out there with her. Since the moment I woke up this morning I've been filled with nausea over this meeting. I don't know why I'm here, I'm only fourteen, just a kid, what could a lawyer possibly need to talk to me about?

My great-grandfather died three weeks ago, but I'm not really sad. Tallulah and I went to the funeral, Mom made us wear matching black dresses and heels, but no one cried like they do in the movies. It was weird; there was hundreds of people there, a sea of black suits and huge sunglasses, but no one really seemed upset.

I didn't know him that well. I know he lived in the city not too far from our house, but apart from once or twice at

Christmas when I was little, I don't actually remember spending any time with him. He sent Tallulah and I cheques on our birthday and Christmas, but other than that he's never been a part of our lives.

Mom and Dad are pissy about me being at this meeting but I don't know why. I overheard them talking about how ridiculous it is that they have to bring me, but neither of them has actually spoken to me about why I'm here. I don't think they know either.

Both Tallulah and I should be at school today, we've only been at St Augustus for a couple of weeks, and not long enough to make any friends yet. I don't like it there; the classes are really hard and it's strange being in a real school when we've been home schooled until now.

When we enter the office, the lawyer motions for us to sit down, and I move to a chair off to the side, behind my parents. No one's taking any notice of me, but I still brush down the back of my skirt and sit demurely in the cool leather chair, placing my hands in my lap just like my etiquette coach taught me. I'm not sure why any of this stuff matters but Miss Phillips is constantly telling me that a young lady should always behave appropriately.

"Thank you so much for coming in today. Firstly, please accept my sincere condolences, Harold and I have been associates for many years and he will be sorely missed," the lawyer says.

I stay silent because I don't think he was talking to me. He's looking at Dad and it was his grandfather that died, so it makes more sense that he was talking to my dad rather than him offering me condolences over a man I barely knew.

"As you're aware Harold's estate is currently valued at a little over twenty billion dollars, including his many businesses and property. I have his last will and testament

2

here and if you're happy for me to proceed I'll go ahead and read it for you," the lawyer says.

"Mr. Worth, shouldn't my father be here for this?" Dad asks.

The lawyer's face turns an odd shade of pink and his lips droop into a frown that makes him look a little like he's going to cry. "Its customary that only the beneficiaries of the will be present at the reading. If you would like to invite Mr. Archibald to be present, we can delay until he is available."

From my seat I watch as Mom glances at Dad, her red polished fingers reaching out to lay a palm across his leg.

"My father isn't named in the will?" Dad asks, his voice shocked.

"Perhaps I should continue to read the contents of the document, hopefully that should answer any questions you might have," Mr. Worth says, his voice calm and monotone.

"Of course," Mom says, in her sickly-sweet tone that she only uses on men. "Please go ahead."

Mr. Worth clears his throat, then opens the sealed envelope from in front of him and pulls out the contents. Methodically he places the envelope back down on his desk and clears his throat again before lifting the pile of papers in front of him. "I Harold James Archibald, resident of New York City in the state of New York, being of sound mind, not acting under duress or undue influence, and fully understanding the nature and extent of all my property and of this disposition thereof, do hereby make, publish, and declare this document to be my Last Will and Testament, and hereby revoke any and all other wills and codicils heretofore made by me."

He pauses, lifting his eyes from the document to glance at me before his gaze drops again and he continues to talk in language I don't understand until my name is mentioned.

"What?" Mom squawks.

"I leave my estate in its entirety to my eldest great granddaughter Miss Carrigan Prudence Archibald, providing she adhere to the attached list of stipulations," Mr. Worth repeats.

My parents' voices become a cacophony of noise and I cringe as they continue to argue with Mr. Worth, my dad jumping up from his seat and demanding to read the will for himself.

I do nothing, and simply sit in my seat without having even the smallest idea that this day would change everything.

PRESENT DAY

S taring down at the cell phone in my hands I read the words of the letter I memorized years ago, the words that my mom made me recite over and over again until I could relay them on demand. The rules. The stipulations that I have to abide by to receive the money my great-grandfather bequeathed to me in his godforsaken will.

Carrigan,

    The Archibald name has been honored and revered for our hardworking nature and upstanding moral values for hundreds of years.

    My child and his child in turn have sullied our family's good name and made a mockery of the fortitude and perseverance our ancestors and I strove so hard to instill. As such I have decided to attempt to make our family great again with your generation.

    I'm worth a great deal of money, all of which will

ultimately become yours if you can prove that you are prepared to work hard to be successful and contribute to the legacy I want to create for the future generations to come.

The world can be a complicated and difficult place to navigate, and as such I have created strict guidelines that I expect you to abide by. This inheritance is not free money. I expect you to work for it and by asking you to abide by this set of rules, I am providing you with the incentive to become a person worthy of being called by the Archibald name.

Should you fail to live up to the standard I expect of you, the bequest will be revoked and my lawyers will act on my wishes on who should inherit in your stead.

Below is a list of my expectations of you as my sole heir.

One – I expect you to graduate as an exemplary student from the school I attended, St Augustus Preparatory School, with no less than a 4.0 grade point average.

Two – You will apply to, and be accepted into, one of the below mentioned colleges.

Harvard University

Cornell University

Yale University

Princeton University

Three – You will graduate from one of the aforementioned educational facilities with a useful degree and no less than a 4.0 grade point average.

Four – As my heir you will create a beneficial alliance through marriage, with a son from a suitable family from the list provided. You will then relinquish control of all of my business assets to your husband who will take over the day-to-day running of my companies.

Five – You will be a person of the upmost moral fortitude, by entering the married state as a virgin. An annual medical examination will be required of you and a report provided to Hallsworth, Hallsworth and Kingston attorneys at Law, until your marriage to ensure you are still untouched.

Six – Unless you are physically unable, you will provide at least one heir to inherit the Archibald fortune upon your death. Should you be unable to have children, the Archibald fortune will pass to the next eligible recipient of my estate, you and your husband will be provided for with an annual stipend until your death.

Seven – You will maintain the honor and status of the Archibald family by being a person of upstanding value and worth. As a wife and mother, you will support your husband and children in any way required and within the expectations of our family heritage.

Eight – You will remain married and faithful for a minimum of twenty years, unless you become a widow, at which point an alternative marriage should be sought from one of the approved family bloodlines. Should it be your wish to dissolve the relationship after this point, if a suitable heir has been created then you may file for divorce and be provided the widows maintenance allowance while the rest of your estate will be passed to your eldest child.

Nine – Upon producing an heir, you agree that your children—should they wish to inherit upon your death—will adhere to also live by these guidelines to ensure the purity of my bloodline and legacy.

Should you not adhere to any of the above listed rules, you will forfeit all rights to my estate. Upon reaching your twenty-fifth birthday, should you decide that you no longer wish to inherit, then you may choose to refuse the inheritance and continue to live your life as you see fit.

I understand that you may feel that these guidelines are extreme, but I fear that without this guidance our

7

family will be lost to laziness and a false sense of expectation that my wealth has given my son and grandson. You, Carrigan, are my final chance to set straight the failings I have encountered in my own children and I hope you succeed and live a happy, prosperous, fruitful life.

Regards,

Harold Archibald the Third.

I can't help the scoff that falls from my lips when I consider the words written by a geriatric old man that have ruled my life for years. I remember the first time I read this letter, I'd laughed, sure that it was all just some elaborate joke. Because what other reason could there possibly be? Who in their right mind would discard their family and leave all their money to a fourteen-year-old on the proviso that she live by a certain set of rules?

By the time my parents and grandparents had screamed and shouted and petitioned the courts to get the will overturned it was too late. The entire world, or at least the world we live in, the world of the filthy rich, all knew that eventually I'd be worth billions. In the blink of an eye I went from being Carrigan Archibald, new girl. To Carrigan Archibald, heir to a fortune.

I'd like to say I handled the new notoriety well, that I didn't let it change me, that my family laughed it off. That they loved me more than the money. But none of that is true.

My parents lost their minds, I lost mine, and somehow everything I've done in the last three and a half years, the way I've lived my life to adhere to that old man's rules, has led me here.

It's my sister's engagement party tonight. She's marrying the boy my parents wanted to be mine. I don't know if I ever really wanted him, or if I was just told I wanted him so many times that I started to believe it.

Arlo Lexington is from the right kind of family. My great-grandfather was a real peach when it came to picking my future husband. With that letter that damned me, he also provided a list of names of suitable husbands for me. They range from twenty years older than me all the way down to five years younger.

I've met them all, flirted with the ones my parents asked me to flirt with, ignored the ones they thought were beneath us. Everything I've done, every thought I've had for the last few years, has been about securing me a husband.

Another slightly crazed laugh falls from my lips and I'm glad that the room is empty, because right now I don't know if I should be laughing or crying or screaming. My life went to shit the day that will was read, but it imploded when I watched my parents beat the hell out of my sister. Physically attack her, punch her, and slap her until she was cowering on the floor at their feet.

That was the moment I knew this was all wrong. That the person I'd allowed the money to make me was evil. That I was evil, that they were evil. But what do you do when you realize that about yourself? It's not like you can just take it back. If I could I'd like to think I would. Or maybe I wouldn't because despite it all, despite all the truly despicable things I've done since I first read that will, I still want the money.

I want the power that comes with it. I want to be wanted, envied, desired, and without that billion dollar pay out I'm just another rich girl.

Now I'm here, planning my own judgement, ruining my future, changing my whole life because I am a terrible person and bad people have to pay a penance for their actions. Today is my penance, my day of reckoning so to speak, and it all started at five o'clock this morning.

SEVEN HOURS EARLIER

"Hey."

I'm jolted to the side as someone shoves me in the shoulder. My eyes snap open and I act on instinct, grabbing the arm of my attacker and throwing them to the side as I jump out of bed and block any further attempts at violence with my forearm across their throat.

My Dad is a survivalist, so me and my brother have been trained in multiple martial arts and forms of both attack and self-defense. We've done survival training in all environments and some pretty heavy-duty war scenario training. My dad is a lovable whack job, but if someone comes at me at least I know I can defend myself.

Blinking past the haze of sleep, I realize that my attacker is a tiny blonde teenage girl. At first I think it's Tally, but the long pink nails clawing at my arm show me that it's not my friend, it's her evil doppelganger.

Releasing my hold on her throat I step back, narrowing my eyes at her. "What the fuck are you doing Crueligan?"

11

"Really you psycho, what am I doing?" she shrieks.

"You're in my room in the middle of the fucking night, but I'm the psycho," I snarl back.

"It's five am, it's hardly the middle of the night and I was trying to wake you up."

"Why?" I demand, taking another step back and crossing my arms across my chest, not caring that I'm completely naked.

Like she's just realized I'm not wearing any clothes, her gaze drops to my dick hanging between my legs. I'm well endowed, I'm not boasting, just stating a fact. I have a big dick and even completely uninterested like he is now, he's still pretty impressive.

"Oh my god, can you put some clothes on?"

"No," I say, pursing my lips.

Her eyes lift comically high, like she's never seen a dick before, and I swear if it wasn't dark in here she'd be bright red with embarrassment. "Look I need your help, okay?"

"What do you want me to help you with?" I ask, suspiciously.

Her sigh is audible as she twists her head to the side, her eyes still focused on the ceiling. "Can we go somewhere away from here to talk, where you have clothes on?"

"Look at me," I demand.

"Why?"

"Because I don't trust a single word out of your mouth, so if you're asking me for something, I want you to be looking me in the face while you do it," I snarl, shocked when she instantly complies.

"I just, I just need your help. Can we please just go somewhere away from my sister so we can talk in private?" she asks, her eyes full of something I don't expect to see. Honesty and fear.

Assessing her for a long moment I nod. "Okay, give me five minutes to get dressed."

Without saying a word, she rushes from my room and I can't help the smile that spreads across my lips. Crueligan is embarrassed, how fucking adorable, the evil one goes shy at the sight of a dick. Less than five minutes later I stroll out of my room and into the dimly lit living room of the hotel suite. Carrigan is waiting for me, sat primly on one of the sofa's wearing the dress she wore yesterday when she, Arlo, and Tally ran from their crazy parents' house.

"I'm ready, where do you want to go?" I ask, my voice low.

"Anywhere we won't be overheard," she says meekly, swallowing thickly as she gracefully rises from the sofa and takes a step toward the door.

"We can go to my boat, the crew won't be there," I suggest, not really wanting her in my personal space but unsure where else we can go that will guarantee privacy.

"Okay," she nods, placing a piece of paper on the coffee table before leading the way out of the room.

Stopping at the coffee table I pick up the note she just left and scan the contents. Placing it back down, I follow her out of the suite, staring at her perfect fucking ass swaying with each step she takes in her stupidly high heels. "How the fuck do you walk in those stilts?"

"Practice," she snaps back, her tone full of snark and vitriol.

"Stop," I demand and she freezes. "Turn the fuck around and look at me."

My dick twitches when she immediately turns all the way around on those stupid heels until she's facing me.

"What?" she asks, her tone bored as if I'm wasting her time.

"Let's get one thing straight here, Priss. I am not one of your little fucking minions. If you want me to help you, then you need to start speaking to me with some respect. I have never been disrespectful to you and I expect the same in return."

Her lips part as shock flashes across her face. Has no one ever called her on her holier-than-thou attitude before? "I'm…" she stutters. "I'm sorry."

"Okay then, let's go," I say, walking past her and toward the elevator.

"That's it?" she asks, her voice unsure.

"That's it. I told you that I wasn't happy with you, I explained why and you apologized. So let's go." I press the elevator call button and a second later the doors slide open. Gesturing for her to go ahead, I watch as she walks forward, her heels clicking on the tile floor. "Do you need to get some clothes?"

"Everything I own is at my house and I don't plan to go back there, so until the stores open I'm stuck with this," she says, gesturing to her tight fitted dress, "or the pajama's Tallulah lent me."

"You kind of look like you're doing the walk of shame, wearing that this time of the morning." I say with a smirk.

Her eyes widen comically large. "I do not."

"Priss, you're in a tight dress and hooker heels at," I look at my watch, "almost five-thirty in the morning, you look like you're getting home from a hook up."

Bringing both hands up to cover her face she shakes her head slowly. "Great," she says, the word muffled.

"We'll stop and find you something more casual to wear, don't worry about it," I say, not hiding the laughter in my voice.

"Where are we going to find a store open at this time in

the morning?" she groans, separating her hands enough that I can hear her words.

"Easy, there's a twenty-four-hour mall near the financial district, we'll go there first, pick you up something to wear and grab some food, then go to the marina to talk."

The elevator dings to tell us we've arrived in the lobby and I reach over and pry her hands free from her face. "Come on, let's go get my car from the valet," I say, keeping hold of one of her hands as I tow her along behind me.

Five minutes later we're inside my Mercedes cruising along the quiet early morning streets of New York, in surprisingly comfortable silence. I don't really know Carrigan beyond the fact that she's set to inherit a fortune. I've never spent more than a couple of minutes alone with her before now. My family is rich but apparently not old money enough to have made it onto her great-grandfather's wish list, so she's never been forced on me the way she has with Arlo.

Until recently I'd considered her to be a heartless, evil bitch and despite her behavior in the last few weeks, I've haven't seen anything that's really changed my opinion of her. For years she's helped her parents hide and enslave Tally, forcing her to give up her own identity so she could pretend to be Carrigan and get her through high school with that all important GPA.

I get that in the world we live in money is important, but fucking hell we're all loaded. My family own an island for fuck's sake. No one ever even goes there, but in the realms of the rich and uber rich owning your own island is a serious boasting point. If we were all poor, I think I could maybe understand the Archibald's single-minded pursuit of this inheritance and Carrigan's willingness to be completely controlled by a dead man's rules. But we're not poor, and for me that's what makes her behavior inexcusable.

Tally is convinced that Carrigan is as much a pawn in their parents' game as she was, but given everything her sister has done in the last few years I think this is all just wishful thinking on her part. She wants her sister to be redeemable and I can understand that, but I don't think she should overlook everything Carrigan's done so easily.

Glancing at the girl beside me, I try to see what Tally sees. I try to consider that just like they manipulated Tally with guilt, they manipulated Carrigan too. I suppose it could be true. The girl's parents are definitely twisted enough to do it. Hell, they tried to drug Arlo so Carrigan could have sex with him and try to get pregnant, all while they recorded it so they could blackmail him if it didn't work.

"Why did you do it?" I ask her, unable to keep the question in any longer.

"What?"

"Why did you fuck Tally over like that? She's your twin sister."

When she doesn't speak I look over to her, she's staring straight ahead, her jaw firm, lips pursed. "Priss I asked you a question."

"Why do you keep calling me Priss?" she demands, swinging her face in my direction. "I have a name."

"I know what your name is, *Carrigan*," I say, enunciating her name sarcastically. "But I think Priss suits you better."

"You're a dick," she hisses, turning back to look out the windscreen again.

"I may be a dick, but you still haven't answered my question."

She sighs and the sound is pained. "It doesn't matter why I did it, I know what you all think of me."

"Just be honest," I snap.

"Fine," she hisses. "When it all started, I didn't know I

16

was doing anything wrong. I was fourteen and terrified of screwing up and losing my family billions of dollars. When I realized that maybe we weren't being fair to Tallulah I was too far into it to turn back. My parents were so sure that it was the right thing to do, that we all had our roles to play and that, that was hers. I guess I had no idea how bad things had gotten or maybe I just didn't want to see until the day they attacked her." Her voice cracks on the last words.

Glancing at her again, I'm shocked to see her hurriedly wiping away a tear from her cheek. I didn't realize she was capable of feeling bad. Honestly, from the moment Tally dragged her out of that party, drunk off her ass, I thought she was just doing this to save her own skin, but maybe there's more to it than just that.

"So all this, trying to break the will, it's for her?"

I feel her turn to look at me, so I risk another glance away from the road. Her eyes are downcast, her teeth worrying her lower lip. "I'd make myself sound better if I said yes wouldn't I?" she asks.

"Not if it's a lie," I say simply.

"Part of it is because of what they did to her, but mostly it's to save myself," she admits quietly, and that honesty, even though it's ugly, impresses me.

"It's okay to look after yourself, to be selfish," I find myself saying, even though I don't necessarily think it's true, at least not all the time.

"Maybe, for some people, but when selfish is one of your defining characteristics I'm not sure it's so acceptable," she says, laughing dryly.

"Is that how you see yourself?" I ask, finding that I genuinely want to know her answer.

"Selfish, stupid, vain, weak minded, yeah pretty much," she says soberly.

"I don't think you're stupid."

"So just selfish, vain, and weak minded then," she scoffs.

"I think we all have the capacity to be all of those things, it's our choices that define us. Maybe what you're doing for your sister now is your chance to be different. Tally think's you're as much a victim in all of this as she is."

"She's wrong," Carrigan says, cutting me off. "I might not have understood what I was doing in the beginning, but in the last couple of years I was fully complicit, I knew what I was doing. I'm not innocent, and I'm not a victim."

With her words we both fall silent and stay that way until we reach the mall and I pull into the underground parking lot. "Come on, let's go and get you something to wear," I say, killing the engine and opening my car door.

Rounding the car, I find Carrigan sitting primly in the front seat waiting for someone to open her door and I can't help but smile at the difference between her and her sister. Tally would open the door, even if you wanted to do it for her, that's just the type of girl she is. Maybe it's because she's been hiding for the last few years, that she's forgotten that's she's an indulged rich girl, but Carrigan hasn't. She's every inch the socialite and I can't help but want to play with her a little.

Standing beside the door I cross my arms across my chest and wait. After a minute or so she looks out the window and spots me standing there. It's obvious I'm not planning to open her door and after a second she looks down at the handle and opens it herself.

"I wondered how long it would take you," I drawl.

"You could have just opened it for me," she snaps peevishly.

"I could have, but I promise you, you're not too rich to open your own door," I say with a smile.

Muttering beneath her breath she stomps away from me, but I don't move.

"Priss," I say, using the nickname I've given her as a demand. I'm shocked, but pleasantly surprised, to see her stop and turn toward me. Tipping my chin in the direction of her still open car door I stand impassively as she rolls her eyes; marching back over to me and slamming the door shut, still muttering what I'd guess are curses beneath her breath.

Smiling to myself I lock my car and stroll after her, enjoying the shape of her bare legs and the way her almost non-existent curves are emphasized by the dress. At first glance her and Tally are completely identical, but now I'm taking the time to really notice there's some obvious differences between them. Tally is curvier, neither girl is fat, but Tally's body is more natural, where Priss looks skinny. In jeans and a tank, she'd be waif like.

The longer I stare, the more dainty she looks and some instinctive urge to feed her comes over me. I'm an active person, my entire family are, but we love to eat. In fact my parents are huge foodies, they love to cook and discover new recipes. I enjoy food, all food. Healthy stuff, and the kind of food that's running with butter and cheese that I doubt a girl like Priss has ever even tasted.

I catch up to her in a couple of strides and when we reach the automatic doors that lead into the mall I'm at her side. Considering it's not quite six in the morning there's plenty of people wandering between the shops and restaurants. "Food or clothes first?" I ask.

"Clothes, although most of these places don't look like my usual style," Priss says, her right arm wrapped across herself as she holds onto her left arm at the elbow.

"Maybe try something different," I suggest. "Your sister mainly wears casual stuff, jeans and shorts."

"Mom would kill me."

"Fuck her! This isn't about your mom. You left remember. Because your parents are fucking psycho's, so who cares if your mom would lose her shit about you buying a pair of jeans. Hell, get a pair just because she'd hate them."

Her eyes lift to look at me and all of her usual superior confidence is gone. In this moment she looks young and terrified.

I move without thought, pulling her to me and wrapping her in my arms while I hold her against my chest. She stiffens, not returning my hug, and somehow that only makes me want to hold her tighter. Both Priss and Tally are fucked up, but where Tally is a fighter, I'm not sure that Priss is, at least not at the minute.

Maybe Tally has been right all along, maybe Priss is just as much a victim of this money and their parents' greed as she was. Either that or she's just an incredibly good actress.

Reluctantly I release her and her timid eyes find mine again, only now they're full of confusion. "Come on Priss, let's go find you something your mom would fucking hate," I say with a smile, reaching for her hand and entwining my fingers with hers, as I tow her toward the first shop I spot with women's clothes in the window.

"What size do you wear?" I ask, not letting go of her hand as I weave in and out of rails, searching for jeans.

"A two."

"Jesus," I murmur, grabbing clothes from rails and then moving her toward the changing room. "Here, try these on," I say, thrusting the piles of clothes into her arms.

"I can't wear these," she says, lifting the tiny pair of black shorts into the air.

"Sure you can, Tally has a pair smaller than that and she looks hot as fuck in them. Just try them on, I've never seen you in anything but school uniform and those tight dresses you seem to like so much."

"I'm not my sister," she spits, glaring at me.

"I am well aware of that Priss. I wasn't suggesting you dress like her, more that as you're fucking identical and she looks good in shorts, you would too. So stop being so fucking difficult and just go and try them," I say, pushing her gently into the changing room and drawing the curtain.

Turning I wander the racks again, grabbing a couple of pretty summer dresses that seem more her style, in case she has a meltdown over the jean shorts, then make my way back to the changing rooms again. "How's it going?" I ask.

"I look weird," she says from behind the curtain.

"Come show me," I say, swallowing the laugh that tries to break free.

Slowly the curtain pulls back and she's standing there, the tight dress gone and in its place, skinny jeans and a pink t-shirt. "You look about twelve," I say, chuckling at how uncomfortable she looks.

"Oh my god," she cries, trying to draw the curtain back.

I reach out and stop her. "The jeans look good on you, but the top is far too third grade." Rooting through the pile of clothes I'm holding, I pull out a fitted white cami top, similar to one I've seen Tally wear in the past. "Try this one instead."

"This is so humiliating, I have a closet full of couture, why are we buying off the rack?" she moans, pulling the curtain closed. "I still look weird," she announces a couple of minutes later as she opens the curtain with a flourish.

"You look hot," I say, eyeing the way the floaty fabric of the shirt clings to her tits and how tiny her waist is in the jeans. It's so small I think I could wrap my hands around her and my thumbs would touch.

She turns to look at herself in the mirror, her brow

wrinkling with distaste. "I think the last time I wore jeans I really was twelve."

"Tally wears jeans."

"Never out in public, Mom says they're the clothes of the working class."

"Priss, your mom is a bitch," I say coldly, hating that Vanessa Archibald ever had a chance to damage both of her daughters so much.

Priss's laugh is high and sweet. "She really is. I look weird but just out of spite I'm buying the jeans because she'd be appalled to see me wearing them. Can we get some sneakers too, and a sweatshirt? Oh and I need a hairband, I want to tie my hair up."

A smile spreads across my lips as I take in her moment of rebellion. It looks good on her, it softens her edges a little and makes me forget, at least for a moment, that she's not as innocent as she looks.

In the end we leave the mall with Priss wearing tiny jean shorts, a white tank, pink converse, and a white baggy hooded sweater, with the jeans and top she tried in a bag dangling from her fingers.

Out of the sexy dresses and six-inch heels, Priss looks younger, sweeter, and sad. There's an innate melancholy in her eyes that I don't think I've ever seen in someone our age before. When Arlo backed Tally into a corner she came out swinging, throwing barbs with her words and making sure that we all knew how pissed she was. But Carrigan doesn't seem to have that fire. I can sense something beneath the perfect exterior, but it's so stifled that I'm not sure it would emerge even if she was really pushed to the edge.

The Archibald's really have done a number on this pair. It makes me wonder if Tally had been the eldest twin how she would have reacted to her parents' manipulations? Would she have let them treat her like a cash cow, or would she have rebelled before it dissolved to threats and violence?

The moment we get into my car, all of Priss's spite driven rebellion dissolves and she becomes quiet and withdrawn. There doesn't seem to be an ounce of fight in her right now. I shouldn't care, Carrigan isn't my friend or my problem, but there's something about seeing a glimpse of fire and then watching it be doused that's affected me. I'm not sure if it's sympathy I'm feeling but I need to be careful. Carrigan Archibald has spent years playing men, toying with them, flirting with them, and generally doing whatever her evil bitch of a mother taught her to do to snag her a husband. She's not above manipulation to get what she wants.

Pulling into a drive through fast food place just around the corner from the marina I turn to Priss. "What do you want to eat?"

She shakes her head. "I'm fine, I normally just have a green juice for breakfast, I'll get something later."

My lips turn down into a scowl. "No."

"No?" she echoes back at me, confusion making her brow furrow.

"No, I'm ordering breakfast, so you'll eat with me. You're skin and bone, you need some proper food in you," I growl.

"I can't eat anything here. Do you know how many calories are in the food they serve here?" Her voice goes up as she finishes speaking and I can almost taste her panic.

"Priss, you can eat whatever you want, you don't have an ounce of fat on you. If anything, you're too skinny. Order a proper fucking breakfast so we can sit down and eat together before we talk."

Her eyes dart to the menu, widening a little, while she shakes her head. "Mom never let us have carbs, I've never eaten most of this food," she says a little shakily.

My lips part to call bullshit, then I remember Tally saying she only ate pizza for the first time when she went to visit family last summer, that their mom said they'd get fat. "I'll get us a bit of everything, you can see what you like and I'll eat the rest, I'm a growing boy," I say with a wink. "Juice, coffee, or both?"

"Juice please," she says meekly, and for the hundredth time this morning I want to punch Vanessa Archibald in the face for being such a cunt. I wish I knew which version of Carrigan was the real one. Is she the docile girl or the conniving, Machiavellian woman?

I order a mix of food; pancakes, waffles, breakfast burritos, eggs, hash browns, sausage patties, and lots of bacon. More food than we could ever eat, but I don't care. Right now I want her to gorge herself on greasy, fatty foods, the stuff that tastes so nice because you know how bad it is for you.

Driving to the marina I pull to a stop in the parking lot opposite my boat. Priss doesn't wait for me to open her door this time, and I smile to myself as she climbs from my car, her new pink sneakers sparkling in the early morning sunshine. Despite the shopping and the stop for food, it's only just after seven and the marina is empty but for a few early risers making the most of a full day on the water.

Handing the bags of food to Priss, I slide the gangplank down onto the pier and secure it in place, then take the food from her and gesture for her to lead the way. More confidently than I expect, she climbs aboard and waits for me on the deck.

"Inside or out?"

"Can anyone hear us out here?" she asks.

"I doubt it, but I suppose if there's anyone on the other boats they might. Inside would definitely be more private."

"Inside then please, I'd rather no one overhear us," she says, her voice timid, her body language so different than her normal superior poise.

"Okay then," I say, pulling my keys from my pocket and quickly unlocking the galley door, gesturing for her to move ahead of me and go inside.

Watching her take in the luxurious interior of my boat, I enjoy the way her eyes roam around the space. I love this yacht, it's my escape, my freedom, and the thing that makes me happiest in the world. My parents are awesome, but they suffer from serious wanderlust and more than a few months in one place has them itching for the next big adventure. They always want to try a new town or country, and as a kid that meant me and my brother packing up and going with them every time they decided to move. Since starting St Augustus, I put my foot down and refused to drop everything and travel with them at their whims, this boat is my only throwback to that transient life. It doesn't matter that I only sail on this lake, it's big enough that the open water feels limitless when I'm out there.

I don't allow many people on here; until Tally came with us, my family and the guys were the only people to step aboard apart from my crew, but for some reason it feels okay to have Priss here with me, and I don't really understand why.

Maybe I'm forgetting who she is because of how she looks, but I need to remind myself how bad a person she is and ignore how much she looks like her sister, a girl I truly adore. In such a short amount of time Tally has become the sister I never had. She's so resilient and just fucking awesome to be around. I love her and I love her for Arlo, they are so perfect for each other, and even though we're young I can see them going the distance.

They might be twins, but Priss isn't her sister and as she

sits primly down on one of the couches I'm reminded of their differences once again. Silently I unload the bags of food onto the coffee table, handing her juice to her and motioning to the food. "Dig in."

A look of panic flashes in her eyes, but it's gone just as quickly as I watch her assess the table full of food in front of us. "The pancakes are the only things I recognize and I can't eat them," she says, that all too familiar disgust filled tone coming back to life.

"Why not?" I ask.

"I just can't," she snaps, taking a tentative sip of her juice.

"Because your mom told you you'll explode if you eat carbs?" I say with a snicker. The silence that follows is telling and I can't help but shake my head in disgust. Stabbing a forkful of pancake, I dip it into the pot of maple syrup and hold it up to Priss's lips. "Try it, I dare you," I say with a mocking raise of my brows.

For a second she freezes, not moving, then I see anger ignite within her. I don't know if it's the mocking, or the fact that I dared her, but her lips part and she opens her mouth eating the food from my fork.

I watch as she chews, her eyes falling shut as the most seductive moan comes from her.

Fuck. Swallowing thickly I wait, desperate to hear the sound again, but it doesn't come. "More?" I say, not sure if I'm begging her to make the sound again or if I'm offering her more food, but either way when she nods, I cut off more pancake and drown it in syrup before holding it up to her lips again.

When she moans again, I swear I almost come in my pants. I shouldn't be this turned on, fully dressed, with a girl I hate, but I am and I need more. Cutting off some waffle I stab a strawberry and feed that to her next, watching as the syrup makes her lips shiny and wishing I could lick it off.

Over and over I feed her bites of all of the different foods, loving how she reacts to them like she's never experienced them before. It's somehow one of the most erotic experiences of my life. Between each forkful I bring to her lips, I take one for myself, sharing a fork with her and wishing I could taste her on my lips.

"No more, I'm full," she says as I stab some bacon.

"You sure?"

"I'm sure. It's going to take me days to burn off all the calories," she cries, as a bright, almost unrecognizable smile graces her full lips.

"Never regret enjoying food Priss, it's one of life's great pleasures," I say, wiping a shiny pebble of syrup from her lip with my thumb and immediately sucking it into my mouth.

Her eyes widen and her tongue bobs out, sliding over her bottom lip, tasting where I just touched her.

"What did you want to talk to me about Carrigan?" I ask, clearing my throat and trying to ignore the lust that's hanging between us.

Her expression instantly sobers and I wish I hadn't said anything, because a mask settles into place over her. The sweet girl enjoying foods her evil mother won't let her eat disappears, leaving the evil twin in her place.

"I want to break the will," she says quickly, her fingers linked together modestly in her lap.

"Okay, do you have a new idea on how we can get around your parents paying off the teachers?" I ask, unsure why she needed to have this conversation away from her sister and the others.

"No. But I know what else I can do that'll end all of this,"

27

she says, her gaze fixed on her hands, pointedly avoiding looking at my face.

"Priss look at me when you're talking to me," I demand.

Her chin snaps up and her eyes lock with mine.

"Thank you. Now explain. What can you do that'll break the will?"

"I want you to have sex with me."

Four

"I want you to have sex with me." Even as the words are coming out of my mouth I can't believe I'm actually saying them, and least of all to Carson Windsor. For the last four years I've had it drilled into me that having sex before my wedding night would literally ruin my life, my parents' life, and my entire future. But here I am now asking a guy, I don't even particularly like, to take my virginity.

"What?" he says, actually jolting away from me, the shock and disgust obvious in his voice.

"I have to be a virgin when I get married, if I'm not I forfeit the inheritance and this is over. Done in a matter of minutes," I say, trying to sound confident and pragmatic, and not like this is as big a deal as it actually is to me.

Despite it being one of the clauses of the will, I actually like the idea of only ever having sex with my husband, but I need to get over that unless I want to end up married to Rupert Overston. My skin actually crawls as I think about letting Rupert touch me, the man repulses me and I'll never, never, agree to marry him, no matter how much money I'll inherit by doing it.

"Is this a joke?" Carson demands, in that tone he keeps using that instantly makes me want to do whatever he tells me to.

"No," I say, shaking my head to emphasize the word.

"You want me to fuck you?"

Flinching at the word fuck, I close my eyes and suck in a slow calming breath. "Yes."

"Why?" he growls.

"Why?" I echo, unsure what he means.

"Why me? Wats offered to fuck you the other week, so why me?"

"Because," I snap, looking away from his probing eyes.

"Priss, you better get those eyes back on mine, I already told you I need you to be looking at me when you speak to me," he snarls.

I don't know why I comply, but I do, instantly looking at him, then immediately wishing I hadn't. His face is granite, his lips set in a hard line, his eyes tight as he watches me.

"I want a reason. Why me? Why not Wats or Olly, or hell, one of the minions who follow you around sniffing at your cunt even knowing they're never going to get a taste."

"Because." I stop, not wanting to admit the truth.

"That's not an answer Priss."

"Because I'd rather it be with someone I'm at least attracted to," I confess in a rush, my cheeks blooming with heat as embarrassment consumes me.

Carson is silent for the longest moment of my life and I'm grateful for the reprieve, but hate that he made me confess it at all. What guy doesn't want easy sex? I mean I know I'm a virgin and that's not great, but still, surely sex is sex to a teenage boy.

"I don't know Carrigan, losing your virginity is a big deal."

"This wouldn't be," I insist. "This is just about breaking the will. Think of it as helping my sister get free of our parents. This is the only thing I can think of that will get me and Tallulah free of them, without me having to get arrested."

"So we just have sex, what if they don't believe you, what if your parents pay off the lawyers or something," Carson says, his voice wary.

"That's why we'd need to record it," I whisper, completely unable to look at him now, no matter what he says.

"You want us to make a sex tape," he says slowly.

"No," I say quickly. "Oh my god no."

"Carrigan if we record ourselves having sex, that's a sex tape," he says drolly.

"All the recording would be is evidence, as soon as the lawyers confirm that I broke the clause I'll destroy it. Hopefully no one will ever have to see it, it's just a failsafe in case my parents figure out what I'm doing. We can make sure that no one knows it's you, that the only person that's identifiable is me," I tell him, trying to sound clinical and detached, and failing. I don't feel detached, I feel panic stricken. I'm not sure if I'm terrified that he'll say yes, or that he'll say no, but either way my heart feels like it's beating out of my chest.

After what feels like an eternity of silence, but was probably no more than two or three minutes, I lift my head to find him watching me, his expression guarded but not full of disgust and loathing like I'd expected.

I know how Arlo and his friends feel about me. They think I'm evil, that I screwed my sister over, that I'm just like my parents. So asking one of them for this favor is more than likely going to result in him telling me to go and screw myself. But I had to try, and Carson was the only one I could imagine touching in that way.

"Okay."

"What?" I exclaim, feeling my eyes widen.

"Okay, I'll have sex with you, but I have some conditions," Carson says, calm and collected.

"What kind of conditions?" I ask warily.

"I'm in charge. You do what I tell you to do, when I tell you to do it."

I nod eagerly. "That's fine, I have no idea what I'm doing anyway," I say a little too quickly, feeling a blush fill my cheeks.

A sly smile crosses his lips and I wonder if I've said something wrong, but dismiss it when he starts to talk again.

"Are you on birth control?" he asks matter of factly.

"Yes, I have the implant, my doctor recommended it to regulate my periods," I say, not sure why I'm spewing verbal diarrhea at him.

"Where? Let me see it," he demands.

Lifting my shirt, I run my finger over the tiny scar and the raised lump that holds the implant.

"Good, then I don't want to wear a condom. I've never taken a virgin before and I want to feel it. I'm clean, and I've never had sex without a condom before, I promise."

"I'm clean too," I say stupidly.

"I figured you would be, what with you being a virgin and all," he laughs.

"Oh, yeah," I say, embarrassment forcing me to look at anything but him.

"One more thing," Carson says.

Forcing my eyes back to his, he waits until he knows he has my attention before he speaks. "One time only."

Nodding I swallow down the nausea that fills my throat. I just negotiated losing my virginity with a boy I don't know that well, who hates me. What the hell am I doing?

He nods, mimicking my action, before a smile tips at the corners of his lips. "Okay then, so when do you want to do this?"

"Now," I say decisively. "The sooner we do this, the sooner I can break the will. It's the engagement party tonight and after last night's disaster with my parents losing their minds, and the fact that I've been ignoring their calls since I left with Tallulah and Arlo, we need to do this sooner rather than later."

"So you want to have sex for the first time right now," he says sardonically.

"I want this to be over," I reply, locking my gaze with his. "I just want this to be over."

Exhaling, the smile falls from his lips and he nods solemnly. "Okay, you stay here. I'll go buy a video camera; cell phones are too easy to hack."

I nod, because I really hadn't thought this far ahead. When my cell rings I jump, startled, before pulling it free from my pocket and immediately rejecting the call when I see my sister's name.

"Who was it?" Carson asks.

"Tallulah. I don't want her to know about this until it's over, okay? I left her a note saying you were helping me to break the will, but she never needs to know what you did to help me. No one ever needs to know."

His stare is unblinking, his lips dipping down into a slight frown as he pulls his own cell out and turns it off, showing me the dark screen. "She won't hear it from me," he says coldly, turning on his heel and marching to the door. "The

33

master bedroom is the second door, I want to find you in there waiting for me when I get back," he orders, as he steps out onto the deck and disappears from view.

Five

CARSON

I just agreed to fuck Carrigan fucking Archibald.

What the hell am I doing?

Every bit of common sense is telling me that I should not be doing this, but my dick is ignoring it all and leading me by the balls to an electronics store, to buy a video camera so we can film me taking her virginity.

The thought is so ridiculous I can barely believe that it's true, but it is. Priss has to be a virgin to inherit and me sliding my dick into her virgin cunt will break the will, and that's the only reason why I'm doing this. To free Tally, so she can get her revenge and keep that money from her parents.

That's the only reason.

It's not that after hearing her moan, and watching her react to everything I tell her to do, that my dick is rock hard for her. It has nothing to do with the fact that the thought of plunging into her untouched pussy is too tempting to resist.

I've fucked my fair share of girls and I enjoy sex as much as the next red-blooded teenage boy. I like the feeling of a hot mouth, pussy, or ass around my dick and I'm not ashamed to admit that. But until today I've never fantasized about it being Carrigan's mouth, pussy, or ass.

Now I am though. Even as I'm walking through the store, my hands full of boxes, all I can think about it how tight and perfect all of her is.

Virgins have never appealed to me in the past. I prefer sex with a partner who knows how to make it good for me, but I'm excited to be her first and I honestly have no fucking clue why.

It takes me less than thirty minutes to get a video camera and tripod and be back at the marina, but now I'm frozen, sitting in my car, staring at my boat like it contains a live bomb, which I suppose it does.

I want to fuck her. I shouldn't because I don't even like her, but despite knowing she's a bad person, despite knowing that this could all be a manipulation, a trick, a game, I still want her.

Needing to calm down I close my eyes and draw in a deep breath, trying to slow my racing heart. The moment my eyelids close, all I can see is images of Priss on her knees while I feed my dick into her mouth and tell her exactly what to do to make me come.

Shit. Snapping my eyes open again I count to one hundred, banishing each dirty, depraved image that pops into my head and refusing to allow myself to fantasize. When my heartbeat finally slows to a normal rate, I open the car door, grab the camera from the trunk, and climb onto my boat, letting myself into the galley and immediately heading for the bedroom.

Opening the door, I find her exactly where I told her to be, sat in the middle of the big bed, the TV playing quietly in the corner.

"Hi," she says, immediately turning all of her attention to me.

Her gaze drops to the bag in my hand and I fight the urge to reach down and adjust my thickening cock. Just knowing that she's in here because I told her to be, turns me the fuck on.

I have a few control issues but usually they only affect me, I don't force my idiosyncrasies onto other people. I always manage to tone it down with the girls from school, let them think they're in charge as they bounce on my dick, but at the back of my mind I'm ordering them around, demanding their complete surrender and compliance.

Priss seems to be the exception to that rule, and I don't think I'm going to be able to stop myself from taking control with her. Something about the way she looks at me, like I'm beneath her but her savior all at the same time, makes the proclivities that I usually fight to suppress, surge to life.

She pulls her lower lip between her teeth and I wish it was me biting her, nibbling on her soft flesh while she does exactly what I tell her to. And she will, I already know that without ever having touched her. Carrigan—Priss—will do everything I ask her to, because I think she needs that control too. Suddenly I don't care that there's a good reason to fuck her, I don't care that this isn't about us, that it's about the greater good. All I care about is that soon I'm going to have her at my mercy, I'm going to own her for as long as it takes, and I can't fucking wait.

"Hi," I say, dropping the bag to the bed and immediately pulling out the tripod, unclipping the legs and extending them to reach the floor.

"Did you get everything?" she asks, not moving closer to the bag, her fingers nervously twisting together in her lap.

"Yeah, the video camera has a few hours' worth of

internal memory, so we can record straight to it and then you can transfer it onto a memory stick or just keep the camera, whatever you need," I say, my hands busily setting up the equipment, my dick more than eager to get things started.

"Okay," she says meekly, and I stop what I'm doing and turn to look at her.

"Are you okay? We don't have to do this if you don't want to. Arlo's already planning to get his families lawyers to check the will over to see if there's a loop hole. I'm sure this isn't the only way to break it Carrigan," I tell her, hating every word that's coming out of my mouth if it means I won't get to touch her, but knowing she needs to be sure.

"No, I'm sure. A lawyer might find a loop hole, but I can't stay in the city while they look. My parents are out of control, they want me to marry Rupert before I finish school, they want me to have a baby," she says, the horror on her face so palpable I almost reach for her, only stopping myself when I remember that we aren't friends. "So this is my only option."

Lowering the video camera to the bed, I sit down on the side and motion to her. "Come here."

She moves forward instantly, then pauses at my side.

"On my lap," I tell her.

Her movements are slow and filled with insecurities, but she does as I ask, crawling onto my lap and sitting stiffly.

"How old were you when your great-grandfather died?"

"Fourteen."

"Did you have a boyfriend?"

She shakes her head.

"Has a guy ever touched you Priss?"

"No," she says, not looking at me.

"Have you ever touched anyone?"

"No."

"Didn't you try to climb Arlo's dick and tell him there were things you could do to him and still be a virgin?" I say harshly.

Her face pales and she moves to climb out of my lap, but I wrap an arm around her waist to stop her. "I asked you a question."

"I…" her lips harden and she lifts her chin, arching her neck imperiously. "I know what things to do, even if I've never done them," she says, sounding like the Carrigan I know and hate.

"And what things are those?"

Wiggling, she tries to get free but I tighten my hold on her. "Sit still," I order, and she complies without thought.

"Whose idea was it to seduce your sister's fiancé, yours or your mom's?"

"I'm not innocent," she cries, her eyes bright and flashing with intensity. "I know my sister wants me to be a victim, but I'm not. I'm a terrible person, I did awful things, just like our parents did."

"I know you're not innocent and I know you're not a good person, but that's not the question I asked you, is it?" I wait for her answer, but she doesn't speak. "Priss."

"Hers, it was hers, but I went along with it, I did it," she says in a rush, her cheeks red and her lower lip wobbling.

Carrigan is a bitch, I didn't imagine that. But unless she's a really fucking good actress, this girl, my Priss, is a fucking mess. She's insecure and sad and guilty, so fucking guilty that's it's oozing out of her, and I feel myself soften a little towards both sides of her.

"You one hundred percent sure you want to do this?" I ask, wanting to make sure, before I let myself get too excited about this actually happening

"I'm sure," she says, her voice quiet but steely.

39

Tapping her knee, I reach up and touch her cheek with the back of my knuckles. "Okay, jump off then and I'll set up this camera."

Her inhale is shaky, but like I expected she moves off my lap and crawls back to the top of the bed.

Five minutes later the camera is set up, the power cord plugged into the wall, just in case, the tripod setup in front of the bed. Now there's nothing left to do but grab the remote and get naked. I've deliberately avoided looking at Priss. I can feel her tension from here, exuding off her in waves, but I can't do anything to comfort her, that's not what this is about. I'm not her boyfriend, this isn't about candles and moonlight and roses. This is fucking. Sex. My dick in her hot, wet, virgin cunt, and I wish I could say I'm not excited about that, but I am.

Climbing onto the bed on my knees, my back to the camera, I pull my shirt over my head and drop it to the floor. I'm not ashamed of being naked, its natural and I know I look good, I work out, and it shows. Her eyes widen comically as she takes in my bare skin and I can't help the smile that slides across my mouth.

"Your turn Priss, take your top off."

She faulters and I tilt my head to the side and assess her. There's a light tremor in her hands as she reaches for the bottom of her shirt and starts to peel it up, revealing inch by tantalizing inch of pale smooth skin.

I swear that time stops, and it's like she's on slow motion because it seems to take an extraordinarily long amount of time until the pink of her bra is revealed. Pink, what is it with this prickly bitch and the pink clothes? I'd expect her to favor black, like her soul, but it's always pink, this soft girly color that screams young and innocent, neither of which I'd associate with Carrigan.

Her breasts are small but pert, and straining at the delicate satin cups of her bra; the hint of a rosy nipple peeking out where the lace edges the top. My mouth waters and I fight the desire to pull her breast free and lap at her nipple with my tongue. To sink my teeth into the sensitive skin and bite down, sucking until she's not sure if she wants to pull away or push closer to my mouth.

Can I make her come just by playing with her nipples? Will they be sensitive, or does she want this to be a mechanical interaction, nothing more than a transaction with the sole purpose of breaking her hymen?

No, I'm in charge. I agreed to do this but only as long as I get to call the shots and sex is about more than just shoving my dick into her, or at least for me it is. I want her mindless, lost to the pleasure I can give her. This is the only time I'll get her, so I need to make an impression.

It's a selfish fucked up thing, but I want her to compare every sexual experience she has in the future with this. I want her to remember me, to remember how she screamed so loud her throat was hoarse. Remember how sore she felt the next day, and not just because I was the first person to be inside her, but because she was well used and satisfied. I want this experience cemented in her brain for the rest of her life and if there's any way to do it, I want a copy of the video so I can remember it too and maybe watch it sometime.

Suddenly time speeds up again and she pulls the shirt over her head. Insecurity fills her eyes as she drops the fabric to the comforter and clenches her hands into fists at her sides, fighting the need to cover herself.

"Beautiful," I tell her, my eyes roving over her torso, as I reach out and brush my fingertip across her hard nipple.

Her exhale of breath is loud and a little of the fear leeches from her eyes.

41

"Bra next," I order, my voice harder than I planned, my control slipping a little.

Lifting her hands she moves to unclip the strap, but I find myself moving before I realize I'm actually doing it. "Stop."

She freezes and I move closer. "I changed my mind, turn around, I want to do it."

Slowly she shuffles around until her back is to me, and I get to see her shoulders and the smooth skin that flows down her spine to the waistband of her shorts. Reaching out I trail a fingertip from the base of her neck, down over her bra strap, all the way down until I reach coarse denim. With the edge of my fingernail I scrape my way back up, not pressing hard, but just hard enough that I can see the mark on her skin.

I deftly unclip her bra, pushing the straps off her shoulders. Her breaths become more visible, and without thought I lean down and press a kiss between her shoulder blades, watching as goosebumps rise across her skin.

"Turn around," I whisper, still a command, but I don't need to be loud for her to hear me and comply. She needs this as much as I do, I don't know how I know it but I do.

Her movement is faster, like she's made the decision to embrace what we're doing, like she wants to do as I say, and then she's facing me. Her eyes glance at the camera behind me for a split second, before all of her attention refocuses on me.

"Shall I take off my shorts?" she asks.

"Not yet. Cup your breasts, offer them up to me."

For the first time she doesn't immediately do as I ask, her hands lift then fall back down twice while I wait unmoving for her to obey. When she does, I smile a barely there smile, leaning forward and capturing one of her nipples between my lips.

I suck hard, loving the gasp it pulls from her lips as I lave at her sensitive tip, alternating between sucking, licking, and nipping, as her breaths become pants and moans and gasps. Her back arches and she pushes herself closer to me, desperate for more. I pull back, enjoying the way her pupils dilate and her eyes become wild and feral, and perfectly out of control.

"Don't stop," she gasps, reaching for my hair and trying to pull me closer.

"Stop, hands by your sides," I snarl, my dick hardening further when her hands fall obediently from my hair. I know that in this moment she's confused and frustrated and probably a little angry, and I love it. I want her out of control, I want her desperate and she's close, but not close enough, nowhere near close enough.

But she will be.

Leaning forward, I pull her other nipple into my mouth. She mewls and I'm not sure if it's relief or need, but I don't care. I tease her, taunting her until her fingers are on my head practically ripping my hair out at the roots as she pulls and yanks trying to force me closer.

"Lie back," I tell her, smiling at her glazed expression. She unfurls like a lazy cat, draping herself back against the pillows; a femme fatale sent to seduce me. I follow her back, pressing kisses against her stomach as I work my way down her body, until my lips are pressed against her pussy through the two layers of clothes that are still covering her.

"I can smell you," I growl, inhaling deeply and scenting her desire, the smell intoxicating. "You want me."

Unbuttoning her shorts, I pull the zipper down exposing her matching pink panties that look so fucking enticing on her, I already plan to steal them as soon as I peel them from her body. Pulling her shorts free, I leave her panties in place so I can see the way she looks spread out for me, just for me.

She lifts her butt without me having to ask and I pull the shorts over her feet and throw them to the floor, not caring where they land.

Placing my palms on the insides of her thighs I roughly part her legs. Her gasp is loud and I smile even wider, loving that I've shocked her, that she's off balance. "You good?" I ask, needing her compliance and to know she's still with me.

"Yes," she rasps, her voice rough.

Burying my face between her legs I inhale deeply, my thumbs pressing into her thighs as she instinctively tries to close her legs. I can feel her watching me, her fingers twisting the fabric beneath her as she fights to stay still, shy but not wanting me to stop. Lifting my head, I watch her as I slide my hand up over her mound and curl my fingers into the waistband of her panties.

Her eyes widen and she exhales sharply as I kneel up between her legs, pushing her thighs together as I drag her panties down, revealing her pussy inch by inch. "No," I snap, when her hands move to cover herself.

"I—" she starts.

"Hands by your sides," I order, stifling my groan when her clenched fists fall down to the bed.

Lifting her legs up, I bend her knees so I can pull the panties free of her feet, shoving them into my back pocket as a memento of today.

She's completely naked, vulnerable to my gaze, panting for breath, her eyes still wide, her hair a mess spread haphazardly across the pillows behind her. She looks the most free she's ever looked and my dick is so hard a soft wind could tip me over the edge and have me coming in my pants.

"Part your legs, let me see," I demand, my eyes narrowed on the space between her legs, hair free, like I knew it would be and for today at least, all mine.

"Priss," I demand, my voice hard when she doesn't do as I ask.

She inhales sharply then spreads her legs wide, no hesitation, like she made the decision and then acted once she had.

Her eyes move to the camera, the one I'd forgotten was even there and I move forward blocking her cunt from view. That's for me, only me, and if I could I'd delete the footage where she shared herself bare, even though hopefully nobody but us will ever know the footage even exists.

"I'm sorry, I forgot about the camera," I say earnestly, looking her in the eyes.

"It's okay, I kind of forgot too," she admits, her voice softer now that some of the lust in her has dissolved.

"It's not okay, so now you get to choose. Do you want me to make you come with my fingers or tongue first?"

"First?" she chokes.

"I'm going to make you come over and over Priss," I tell her, rubbing my thumb in circles over the soft skin at the top of her thigh.

"But why? You don't even like me."

"It doesn't matter how I feel about you. You asked me to do this and I am. I told you it would be my way, that I was in control and this is how I plan to do it. I want to own you. Until this is over I want your soul to belong to me. I don't want you to even think unless I've told you to do it. I want you mindless, boneless, and consumed. I want to hear my name fall from your lips and have it be the only thing you know how to say, because the only thing that exists to you is me."

Her lips part and a ragged gasp is the only sound she makes.

"Is that what you want? If it's not we can stop this now,

but if you do, if you want to fall down this rabbit hole with me, if you want to give yourself over to me until this is done, then say yes. I need to hear the word."

"Yes," she says, and a single tear rolls down her cheek.

I can't help myself, I lean down and lick the tear from her skin, because it's mine, all of her is. "Fingers or tongue, or do you want me to decide?"

"You decide, I... I don't... You decide," she mumbles, her words rushed.

I chuckle, I can't help it. "Put your heels on the bed and hold your knees back."

She does exactly as I ask and I dive in, licking at her clit while she almost jumps off the bed, her back arching as she lets out a shocked mewl that makes my dick ache. I eat her, lapping up her taste as I slide a single finger into her sex, loving how tight she is.

She's wet, her body excited and I preen that she's so aroused for me, as I suck on her clit. I wind her body up, touching her, listening to the way her breath increases, the tiny moans she makes as I hit that spot inside of her that makes liquid heat roll down my hand, coating me in her arousal.

Her first orgasm comes out of nowhere and she screams out in pleasure, her cunt tightening around my fingers as I smile against her sex. Not stopping I slide in a second finger, stretching her as I flick my tongue faster, not giving her body a chance to relax before she's hurtling toward a second orgasm. This time her entire body arches, her muscles tense as she cries my name, her voice ragged and fucking perfect.

"Carson," she cries again, her muscles twitching as wave upon wave of pleasure courses through her.

"One more Priss, then I'm going to fuck you, but I need to watch you come once more," I tell her, my own voice nothing more than a rasp as I move upwards. My fingers are sliding in and out of her pussy and I carefully add a third finger, stretching her. She's so wet that my hand is coated in her arousal and her scent has consumed the room, my mouth filled with the taste of her sweetness. Taking one of her nipples between my lips I suck and bite, rubbing my thumb over her clit as I fuck her with my fingers.

Writhing beneath me, her body moves instinctually, her hips grinding against my hand, riding my fingers as her pussy continues to clamp down on me. I want to push her higher, see how much I can get her to give herself over to me. I want to touch her everywhere and drive her wild with my thumb in her ass, my fingers in her pussy, and my tongue on her clit, but I don't want to let her slip off this cliff of pleasure she's atop of.

I want my dick inside her more than anything else, so I tamp down my desire and instead double my efforts to make her orgasm again, tipping her over the edge when I pinch her clit and bite her nipple, basking in the scream that escapes her lips.

"I need to fuck you now, you good with that Priss?" I ask, rolling up onto my knees and quickly unbuttoning my jeans, pushing them off, leaving me naked, my dick rock hard, precum dripping from the tip.

"Priss," I say again, my voice stern, needing to hear her consent.

"Yes, god yes," she pants, her eyes closed, her chest heaving, her nipples pink and swollen.

"Thank fuck," I rasp, positioning myself between her legs. Grabbing my dick, I slide the head between her folds, coating myself in her arousal before I grip her thighs, pulling her closer, and let myself slide into her.

She's hot and wet and so fucking tight that I barely get the head of my cock inside of her before she clamps her muscles trapping me. "Relax Priss," I growl.

I didn't realize it was possible but my dick actually gets harder when her eyes snap open at my command and her gaze locks with mine.

"Let me in," I say, thrusting a little and waiting as she exhales slowly and the vice grip she has on my dick loosens slightly. "That's it, good girl," I praise, pushing in deeper until I hit the barrier of her virginity.

"So tight, fucking perfect," I praise, moving my thumb to her clit and rubbing circles over the tiny bundle of nerves. Her breathing hitches, that hint of discomfort being replaced with lust as I feel wetness pulse around my dick. I want to slam forward, to take her hard and fast, to fuck her like I hate her. But I'm not that much of a bastard. Instead I tell her all the dirty, depraved things I want to do to her body, until she's on the verge of another orgasm, then I pull out and thrust forward, filling her in one movement until her cunt is full of my dick.

Her eyes close as she hisses with the pain, a tear rolling down her cheek and landing on her lips that are clenched together in a hard line.

"That's it Priss, just breathe, you're such a good girl, you've taken my dick so fucking perfectly," I coo, giving her a minute to get used to the feeling of me inside of her before I move.

After a second her face begins to relax and I carefully pull out and gently slide back into her. "Open your eyes," I order. Fuck she's perfect. Her eyes open and she stares at me, trusting me completely in this moment even though we're practically enemies. I keep moving, careful, shallow thrusts that make my balls ache with the need to take her properly.

Taking a tight hold of my control I fuck her gently,

waiting until her pupils dilate again with pleasure and all of the pain is gone from her face. "Bend your knees, lift up your legs, and hold them up with your hands," I growl. Just like I knew she would, she complies and I reward her by leaning down and taking her nipple into my mouth.

Then I start to fuck her properly, rolling my hips as I thrust in and out of her, not as violently as I'd like, but harder than I should. "God yeah," I rasp. "I can feel your cunt fluttering around me. You want to come on my dick don't you Priss, you want to milk my cock and make me fill you up with my cum."

Her reply is nothing more than a garbled moan as her head thrashes from side to side and her fingers hold on to me tightly like she thinks me stopping right now is even an option. I growl, the sound a primal noise that I've never heard before as I fuck her faster, harder, rubbing her clit as I plough into her, needing her to come before I do.

"Come on Priss, scream for me. I want you to scream my fucking name while I own your cunt," I snarl, demanding her compliance.

"Ahhh," she whines.

Leaning back I lift her ass up off the bed, gripping her tightly as I pull her on and off my dick. When she tenses I know she's close. My thumb finds her clit and I circle, once, twice, and then she screams. Her pussy clamps down on my dick, making me come so hard I cry out as she spasms around me. Her cunt pulses, trapping my dick in a vice grip, and I come hard until every drop of cum is drained from me and I fall forward panting and gasping for air.

"Oh my god," Priss rasps, letting her legs fall to the sides as she covers her sweating face with her hand, her body becoming lax.

Carefully I pull out of her, watching my cum drip from

her cunt and both hating and loving the feeling of ownership that fills me. Falling to her side I drag her to me, needing to have her close to me while our breathing settles and our bodies cool. That was the most intense sexual experience of my life.

My eyes fall on the camera still recording at the end of the bed and I grab the remote and turn it off. I need a copy of that video. Priss is silent, her head resting on my chest and I want to hold her close, to kiss her and tell her how fucking perfect she is, but now that it's done and she's no longer a virgin it feels wrong to do something so intimate. Instead I lift my hand and stroke my fingers through the strands of her honey blonde hair, closing my eyes and basking in this moment, knowing that soon it will all be over.

I don't know at what point I fall asleep, but when I wake up my body feels sticky with a mix of dried sweat and the results of the sex I just had with Carson Windsor. The hot, strange, painful, wonderful, world ending sex.

I've known for years that I wasn't going to get to have the casual sexual relationships normal people my age have. I've built up this idea of how my first time would be in my head; knowing that it was unlikely I'd be in love with the first person I shared my body with. I'd assumed it would be awful, that I'd be nervous and mentally distanced from the act, that it would just be one more thing to endure to get the inheritance.

But what just happened with Carson was nothing at all like I'd imagined. I'm not a total weirdo, I've touched myself, explored my own body to see what feels good. I've given myself orgasms, or at least I thought I had, but they were nothing like the way Carson made me feel.

This boy that I don't like, who doesn't like me, made me orgasm so hard my entire body shook, and he didn't just do it once, he made me come four times. Four times! I've never even gotten close to twice in a row on my own and he just kept making me scream over and over.

The actual sex part hurt, at least at the start, but by the end it was amazing, so unlike anything I could ever have imagined and now my body feels sore and relaxed all at the same time. Closing my eyes for a second, I bask in the feel of his chest beneath my cheek. I shouldn't be cuddling with him, this was just about ridding me of my virginity and breaking the will, but I can't help feeling close to him right now.

I always assumed I could make sex just something else to deal with, like every other aspect of my great-grandfather's will, but I was wrong. Even though he didn't kiss me, everything about what we just did was intimate and I was an idiot to think it wouldn't be.

Five more seconds and I'll move. I'll get up, take a shower and wash my body clean of him, then I'll leave. Keeping my breathing steady and even, I try not to wake him. For at least the next few moments I need to pretend that he doesn't hate me, that he doesn't know how terrible a person I am. I need to pretend that we had sex, that I gave him my virginity, because we care about each other and not because I literally didn't have any one else I could ask.

Sighing wearily I move, trying not to wake him as I peel my naked body from his. Wincing slightly as the soreness between my legs, my movements are slow and careful. When I glance down at the boy in the bed I'm surprised to find his eyes open and watching me, but he doesn't smile and he doesn't say anything when I grab my discarded clothes from the floor and cross the room to the bathroom.

The hot water washes away the blood and dried semen from my inner thighs and I cringe at how beat up I feel considering all I did was lie on my back and let him do all the work. A blush fills my cheeks as I remember the things he said to me, the things he said he wanted to do to me. I've never really thought about dirty talk, I guess I never considered the guy I would end up married to would be like that, but I can't deny how much it turned me on.

Everything Carson did turned me on. Before my sister got involved with Arlo Lexington, I'd never said more than three words to Carson Windsor. I've always known who he was, his family are on the list. But either my parents decided they didn't want his family or his family weren't interested, because my mom has never even mentioned him in terms of a potential husband.

There's shampoo and body wash already in the shower and I use them, skimming my hands over my skin and letting my mind wander to the way he touched me. He could have just got me naked and had sex with me, it's what I'd been expecting, but he took care of me.

"I want to own you. Until this is over I want your soul to belong to me." His voice drifts into my head and I have to swallow past the lump in my throat.

He warned me, but I was too far gone to heed his words. He did what he said he would, he owned me. The scary thing is that I think a small part of me will always be his now, that when he took my virginity, he took a tiny part of me with it and I'm not sure I'll ever get it back, or if I even want to.

Turning off the water I search for a towel, eventually finding a pile of clean, black, fluffy ones in a closet and wrapping one around myself. I allow myself a moment to dwell on everything that's happened so far today and how much more will happen before the day is done. Then I dry myself off, redress in the clothes Carson and I bought this morning, minus the panties that seem to have gone missing, and then walk out of the bathroom with my head held high.

The bedroom is empty when I enter it and I freeze,

expecting to find Carson still in bed, his impassive face watching me. Scanning the space my eyes fall on the tripod. The camera has gone too and fear bursts to life in my stomach. He wouldn't take the video, would he?

No. He wouldn't do that. He wants me to break the will for my sister, he wouldn't take the only proof I have that I'm no longer a virgin. Opening the door, I walk into the living room and the breath I'd been holding bursts from me in a relieved huff as I spot him sitting shirtless on the couch, the video camera in his hands.

His body is unbelievable, I noticed it earlier when he took his shirt off, but there's something about watching him like this that makes him even more attractive. He's beautiful. Short deep auburn hair so dark I'd always thought it was brown until today when he was above me, his body joined with mine.

His jaw is covered in a light stubble a few shades lighter than his hair but it does nothing to disguise how strong it is. He doesn't look like an eighteen-year-old boy, he looks like a man, and I have to swallow down the desire that's sparking back to life within me.

Frozen in the doorway I notice he's wearing grey sweatpants now, not the jeans he took off earlier, and his chest is a bare expanse of smooth, hard muscle except for a tattoo over his heart. Honestly I'm not a fan of tattoos, years of listening to my mother's disgust at them has tempered my opinion, another thing I didn't realize her influence has affected.

But I've never actually seen a tattoo on a real person before either. If I knew him better, or at all, I'd cross the room to him and ask to look at it properly, from this distance I'm not even sure what it is, all I can make out is that it's colorful, reds and blues and oranges.

He hasn't noticed me yet, his eyes are on the camera in his hands, his lips parted slightly as he watches. It's only then that I realize he's watching the tape of us. Horrified, my feet move without thought and I march toward him, snatching the camera from his hands and clutching it to my chest, fumbling to turn the video off.

"What are you doing?" I cry.

His smile is slow and languorous. "You know what I was doing Priss. Sit, we can watch it together."

"No," I gasp, mortified by the idea of watching a video of us having sex. "It's bad enough that it even exists. That it even happened. I never want to watch it," I shout, my voice becoming cold and angry, and so much like my mother's that I internally cringe at the sound.

"Wow it didn't take long for that sweet nervousness to wear off did it," he drawls, leaning back on the sofa, his body language mockingly relaxed, like he doesn't have a care in the world. "For a minute I thought a good fuck had mellowed you into becoming an almost decent person, obviously I was wrong."

Inhaling sharply I'm surprised by how much his barb hurts. But it shouldn't surprise me. We're nothing to each other, not friends or lovers and this was just sex. An act between two consenting adults, a means to an end. "We both know I'm not a decent person Carson, a few orgasms was never going to change that," I barb back, hating myself, but needing the familiar mask of superiority to hide behind.

Crossing to the other side of the living room I sink down into one of the couches and look at the video camera. My hands shake as I check that the video is still there, playing it for a second to make sure it works before turning it off and placing it in my lap. I can feel his eyes on me, but I don't look at him. Now this is done I just need to get away from here, away from him and all these feelings that are swirling around inside of me.

Pulling my cell out, I click into the Uber app and order myself a cab, relieved when it says that the driver will be here in less than five minutes. Rising gracefully, I ignore Carson's probing gaze as I make my way back to the bedroom.

The blood stain on the bedsheets immediately grabs my attention, I hadn't noticed it when I came out of the bathroom earlier but now it's all I can see. Bright red against the white sheets. My eyes widen as I fixate on it. I'm not a virgin anymore. Despite knowing that it happened, feeling it in my body, and having a video to prove it, until this moment as I stare at the evidence on the sheets, I hadn't really processed that I had sex.

My chest tightens as panic swells inside of me and before I even realize what I'm doing I'm ripping the sheets from the bed and balling them up as small as I can get them. Grabbing my shoes and purse I hold them to my chest as I rush from the bedroom. "I'm going to find a trashcan," I announce, as I rush past Carson and make a beeline for the door that leads onto the deck of the boat.

Dropping my shoes to the floor I shove my feet into the ridiculous pink sneakers and move, descending the slim gangway that leads down onto the marina. Trying to maintain what little dignity I have left, I rush to the huge dumpsters on the other side of the parking lot, open the lid, and throw the sheet inside before slamming it closed again.

With my eyes tightly shut, I suck in a sharp gasp. I need to leave, to get away from all the tension that's inside that boat with Carson. My cell beeps and I glance down at the screen, almost crying with gratitude and feeling a layer of tension fall away from me when I realize it's a text telling me my Uber driver has arrived.

Glancing back at Carson's boat I find him stood on the deck watching me, his arms crossed over his bare chest, his expression hard and shuttered. Lifting my hand in the biggest asshole move ever, I wave at him, "Thank you for the help," I shout, then I turn and exit the marina, climbing straight into the waiting cab without looking back.

Seven

CARSON

EST 1917

What the fuck just happened? Did she seriously just say, "Thank you for the help," and then leave without another word? My eyes are still trained on the marina entrance, the one she just left through after she climbed straight into a waiting cab, after throwing my bedsheets in the dumpster.

How the hell did things get so fucked up, so fast?

Twenty minutes ago she was asleep, naked on my chest, my cum drying on her freshly devirginized cunt, and now she's gone without anything other than a 'Thank you for the help'.

Anger courses through my veins until I'm pacing the deck, my hands balled into fists at my sides. I knew she was a cold-hearted bitch, but this, this is beyond anything I thought she was capable of. Forcing my feet to stop moving, I shake my head. This is exactly what I should have expected. Carrigan Archibald is a manipulative, calculating bitch. She needed something from me and now she doesn't, simple as that.

I need to stop thinking this was more than it was. She

asked me to help solve a problem and I did. It was just sex. Fucking out of this world, blow my mind sex, but it was still just sex.

Except touching her and feeling the way her tight pussy clung to my dick was epic. Watching the video like a voyeur as she cried out my name, her body writhing beneath me, completely under my control, is quite possibly the hottest thing I've ever seen. Better than even the filthiest of porn I've ever watched.

I shouldn't have sent a copy of it to my cell, but I just couldn't help myself, because the thought of her deleting it after she breaks the will is unthinkable to me. I'll never tell a soul I have it, but I'll know, and I already know I'll watch it again.

Unwilling to wash the smell of sex and her off my body I don't shower, instead I pull on a shirt and slide my feet into my sneakers before cleaning up the food bags and locking up. Once I'm in my car I pull out my cell to text her and realize I don't even have her cell number. A wry laugh falls from my lips and I slam my palms against the steering wheel in frustration.

Without starting the engine I climb back out of my car dialing Matthew, the head of my regular staff who crew the boat when I want to go out sailing.

"Mr. Windsor," Matthew answers.

"Matthew, I know it's short notice, but I want to go out, how quickly can you get here?"

"You pay us to be on call Mr. Windsor," Matthew says with a laugh. "I'll see you in thirty minutes."

"Thank you," I say on a relieved breath, ending the call and making my way back over to 'The Escape', my beautiful boat, my one true love, that's now tainted with the most intense sexual experience of my life.

Securing the gangway in place again I climb aboard and unlock the galley door. The smell of sex and Priss hits me the moment I step inside and my dick instantly hardens. Fuck, once isn't going to be enough. I might hate her, she might hate me, but she's everything I wasn't willing to admit I need in a woman. Perfectly, willingly submissive, happy to let me lead, knowing that I'll make it good for her. She trusted me completely and that feeling, being in complete control of someone else's body, was euphoric.

God, imagine all the things I could do to her now I don't need to be careful with her, all the things I could teach her. We don't need to be friends or in a relationship to fuck, in fact I can totally get on board with a fuck buddy situation—non-friends with benefits so to speak.

My dick throbs at the idea of being inside of her again. She might not know it yet, but this isn't over. I might have said only once, but one taste wasn't enough, and fucking Carrigan Archibald out of my system just became my new obsession.

PRESENT

A quick google search and three phone calls is all it takes to find a gynecologist willing to see me at short notice. The Uber driver pulls to a stop outside of the modern skyscraper where the doctor's office is located and I inhale slowly, trying to calm my erratically beating heart. I didn't give them my real name when I booked the appointment. It's probably ridiculous to imagine that my parents might have been able to find out about this appointment and bribe the doctor, but I didn't want to take any chances. I need to do this today, while my resolve is still firm and before my parents have any clue what I'm doing.

Handing the driver a tip, I climb out and head for the doors, wishing that I wasn't wearing these clothes that made me feel rebellious this morning, but now just feel infantile and ludicrous. My hair is still a little damp, drying into my natural waves that I usually straighten into oblivion before I leave the house each morning. I feel unprepared for this meeting without my armor of designer clothes and flawless makeup but I push forward regardless, because if I don't, I'm not sure I'll ever find the courage to do this again.

I ride the elevator up to the twentieth floor and push open the heavy gold framed glass door that leads into the doctor's reception.

"Good morning, can I take your name?" the receptionist asks politely.

"Priss Windsor," I say, refusing to consider why the fake name I gave, is Carson's surname and the nickname he gave me.

"The doctor is just with a patient at the moment but I'll let her know you're here as soon as she's finished. Please take a seat, can I get you a drink?"

"A glass of water would be great, thank you," I say, forcing a brittle smile to my lips as I turn and take a seat on a comfortable leather chair. Inhaling long slow breaths I try to calm my racing heart. Until this moment I've tried to be pragmatic about this part of my 'breaking the will' plan, but now that I'm here in a strange doctor's office waiting to be examined, I start to panic.

If I was closer to Tallulah, or if my friends were real friends—not people that my parents wanted me to befriend, or people who thought it would benefit them to be friends with an heiress—then I wouldn't be here alone. The thought of having anyone in my life who I trust enough to have my back at a time like this, seems almost comical to me. I literally can't name a single person who is interested in me for purely altruistic purposes. Not even my sister and she truly is a good person, but even she wants something from me.

If I wasn't the key to cutting this noose around both of our necks would she want anything to do with me? I doubt it and I wouldn't blame her.

This isn't the first time I've sat waiting for an exam just like the one I'm going to request in a minute, in fact this will be the fifth one of these humiliating tests that I've had to endure. The first time I was fourteen years old and the doctor my parents took me to was a man. Fourteen years old and hooking my legs into stirrups so a fifty-year-old doctor could confirm that I was in fact still a virgin.

A shudder of revulsion cascades through me when I think about that day, how my mom made me go into the room alone, how scared I was and how ashamed I felt after it was over.

"Miss Windsor, if you'd like to come through," a female voice says, jolting me from my thoughts.

Rising from my seat, I follow the smiling nurse out of the reception room just as the receptionist returns with my glass of water. The nurse leads me down a hallway, opening a door for me and gesturing for me to enter first. She closes the door behind herself and then picks up a clipboard from the counter.

"Miss Windsor," she starts.

"My name is actually Carrigan Archibald. I apologize for the subterfuge, but I need to make sure that no one knows I'm here. My situation is a little, delicate," I say, forcing a polite smile to my lips.

"Oh, err, okay," the nurse says, her eyes widening a little. "Well the doctor will be in to speak to you shortly, there's a gown on the bed, so if you could get changed then fill out these patient forms for me please."

"Thank you," I say, reaching for the clipboard and then waiting for her to leave before quickly undressing and pulling on the blue paper gown. Climbing onto the end of the examination table, I lift the clipboard up and start to fill in the form wondering how much information I can leave blank if I'm paying cash.

A decisive knock on the door draws my attention and I lift my head just as the handle turns and a woman enters the room. "Hello Miss Archibald, I'm doctor Nestor, what can I help you with today?"

"Thank you for seeing me on such short notice," I say, lowering the clipboard to my lap. "I have a somewhat unorthodox problem that I'm hoping you might be able to help me with," I say, cringing as I try to decide how to word this.

The doctor laughs. "Trust me I doubt there's anything you can ask that I haven't heard before."

A scoff falls from my lips. "I wouldn't be so sure about that," I say, then I start to explain about the will and it's the stipulations. I don't tell her everything, just enough that she gets the gist. "So I'm here today because I need you to examine me."

"To confirm you remain a virgin?" the doctor interrupts.

"No, to confirm that I'm not a virgin anymore."

To her credit the doctor's only reaction is a raise of a single eyebrow.

"I need written confirmation that my hymen is no longer intact that I can use as evidence," I say, unable to meet her eyes now.

"You want me to write a letter to confirm you're no longer a virgin?" she asks slowly.

"Look, I don't want this money. You might not understand that, I'm sure most people would think I'm crazy. But I need to break this will because the clauses tie my life up in knots, they keep me bound to its stipulations until I'm twenty-five. This is the only way out. So can you help me, or do I need to find another doctor?" I say, forcing myself to look her in the eye and not back down.

Her nod is slow and unsure to start off with, then her

movement becomes more decisive. "Yes, I can help. With your permission I'm going to ask my colleague to witness the exam and then she can also provide a written confirmation, two independent statements will be beyond question."

A gasp of relieved breath bursts from me. "Thank you," I say, my voice cracking a little.

From then on, she's all business. She leaves the room for a moment, returning with another woman a little older but polite and professional. The exam only takes a moment and then they leave me to get dressed. The nurse from earlier collects me and leads me into the doctor's office and I sit in the chair before her desk and wait.

"Miss Archibald," Doctor Nester says, as she pushes open the door behind me. Instead of circling behind her desk she sinks down into the chair next to mine, inhaling sharply as she smiles. "Here are the letters that you require. I can't say that I completely understand the complexities of your situation but I understand fear and desperation, and Carrigan, I see both of those things in you. There are agencies and people in place to help."

I cut her off. "I appreciate your concern but this letter is all I need at the moment. Thank you for your help today." Lifting my hand, I hold it out, waiting for her to give me the envelope with the paperwork that will change my life.

With a sigh she passes it over and I quickly pull the letters free and scan the words. I close my eyes for a second, relieved, then I open them again and smile at her. "Thank you," I say, offering her my hand.

She takes it squeezing slightly as we shake and then I rise from my chair, the letter held tightly in my hand, and leave. After paying, I ride the elevator down to the street, sliding the letter into my purse alongside the video camera. Exhaling raggedly, I tighten my hold on the strap of my purse, only one more stop to go and this should all be over.

The sun warms my skin the moment I step outside and I tip my head back and allow myself a second to just enjoy the feeling, but a moment's all I get, because I'm almost done, this is almost over.

Lifting my hand into the air I flag down a cab, climb in, and settle back into the seat. I have one more place to go before I head to my sister and Arlo's engagement party, and once again, I wish she and I were closer. If we were, maybe we'd be doing this together. Instead I'm alone, because everything about me is orchestrated, fake, manufactured.

My cell buzzes in my purse, another missed call or text message from my parents. I'm glad that I figured out a way to stop them from tracking my cell phone, else I wouldn't be able to evade them and by now they must know something is wrong. I've only ever stepped out of line once since this all started years ago.

The day I should have attended a dinner at Arlo's house, I turned off my cellphone and went on a date with a cute bartender. I thought for a moment that he liked me, that he wanted me, just Carrigan, but in the end he knew about the money and was hoping to use me as his meal ticket.

My mom laughed when she found out where I was when Tallulah took my place that day. I expected her to go mad, but she just laughed and reminded me that the only reason I was useful to anyone, was because my name was on that will.

Sometimes I like to try and decide if my parents are the worse or if I am. They got side stepped, missed out on their chance at a fortune, I can almost understand them doing whatever they could to get it, even if they got access through me.

But I'm truly despicable, because I was a child and I still

66

did all these things even though deep down I knew they were wrong. I wasn't blinded by greed or need, I've never gone without anything my entire life. So what's my excuse? I don't have one, I'm just bad, just a really bad person.

I wish what I was doing now was truly selfless, that my actions were solely to release my sister from the shackles of obligation, but that would be a lie too. Trying not to ruin her life any more than I already have is definitely part of it, at least something inside of me wants to help her, but the biggest part of my motivation is to save myself.

With Arlo engaged to my sister, my parents moved onto the next boy on the husband wish list, only he's not a boy, he's a thirty-five-year-old man. I don't even know him. I mean I've met him, I've met them all, from choice number one all the way down the list I've been introduced, stood in the same room. But I don't actually know any of them.

Rupert Overston is business mindedly brilliant, rich, and successful. He's also bisexual, predatory, and disgusting. This is the man my parents have arranged for me to marry.

Parents.

Freddie and Vanessa hold that title in the very loosest of terms. Before the will, they travelled and their two children brought nothing but inconvenience to the lavish lifestyle they preferred, and that was okay. Tallulah and I were raised by a series of nannies and tutors. I'm sure we weren't the first rich kids to have absentee parents and we won't be the last.

But after the will, everything changed. My every move became their decision. Every step I took had to be orchestrated, considered. The length and color of my hair, my speech, my makeup, the clothes I wore, the people I associated with. All of it became so much more important than me.

Perhaps if I'd grown up differently I'd have seen their

actions for what they were, controlling. But to a fourteen-year-old girl who had gone from seeing her parents three or four times a year to suddenly having them there every day, basking in me, doting on me, it was invigorating.

I loved the attention, loved that it wasn't about me and my sister, that it was all about me, only me. It didn't matter that she was smarter, more poised, more beautiful with those strange purple eyes. I was the important one.

If I had even a shred of decency left in me I'd be ashamed of myself, but I think I've become so deadened inside that I don't really feel anything anymore, least of all shame or remorse.

I imagine by now my parents must have figured out that I'm trying to break one of the will's clauses, but neither of them has said a thing. Maybe they really don't know, maybe whoever they've paid off at school to make sure I maintain my grades hasn't told them that I'm making a concerted effort to fail.

Maybe my parents are conceited enough that they believe they're reach is infallible, that there's no way anyone would go against their will. At St Augustus that might be true, all the staff seems to be under their thumb, or on their payroll. If I could have just gotten one D this would all be over by now, I wouldn't have had to resort to desperate measures, to begging a boy who despises me to have sex with me.

A shudder runs across my skin as my memory teases me with thoughts of Carson and all the things we did. I'm not repulsed, I'm wanton, turned on by the way I can still feel his touch, feel the soreness between my thighs from his body.

My eyes fall to the video camera in my purse, if I were to turn it on I could see it, relive every touch, every moan, every orgasm. Shutting my eyes I bite my lip hard, using the pain to banish all thoughts of Carson away. It was just an act, just sex, nothing more than the mechanics of intimacy between two people, I can't forget that.

When the cab slows to a stop outside the brownstone that holds the offices of Hallsworth, Hallsworth and Kingston attorneys at Law, I suck in a low shaky breath. I haven't been here since the will was read, but I can still remember that day so clearly.

Tapping my credit card against the card reader I pay the cab driver and climb out, pausing for a minute on the sidewalk, needing to compose myself before I go inside and change my future entirely.

I haven't called ahead, but I know they'll see me, I just hope they don't contact my parents the moment I walk through the door. With my resolve hardened I climb the steps and press the buzzer.

"Hallsworth, Hallsworth and Kingston," a voice says through the speaker.

"Carrigan Archibald to see Mr. Worth please."

There's a pause, then the speaker crackles a second before there's a click and the door lock disengages. Wrapping my fingers around the cool brass handle, I push the door open and step into the dark-wood paneled hall, following the same route I took almost four years ago.

The last time I was here I didn't realize how monumental my visit would be, but this time I'm completely aware that the outcome of today's meeting will change the trajectory of my future entirely. I'm scared, but determined, and that's what pushes me forward and into the small waiting room that houses an antique desk, with a stern-faced man in round horn-rimmed glasses sitting behind it.

"Miss Archibald, do you have an appointment?" he asks brusquely.

"I don't, but I'm confident Mr. Worth will make time to

talk with me once you let him know that I'm here," I say succinctly, using the tone of voice my etiquette coach spent years forcing me to perfect. It's the tone that says I'm better than you, richer than you, and more powerful than you. It's the tone that gets a person whatever they want in life. It's the tone my mother always uses, the tone she taught me to use, the tone I've never heard coming from my sister's mouth, and the tone that will make sure this man doesn't refuse me.

Just like I knew he would, the man lifts the phone on his desk to his ear, presses a button, and then speaks quietly into the receiver. A moment later he lowers the phone back into the cradle and stands. "Let me show you to Mr. Worth's office."

"Thank you," I say politely, and follow as he leads me out of the reception area and toward the offices.

The lawyer's office is identical to how I remember it and a horrible sense of de-ja-vu hits me. Nerves make me want to shake, but I refuse to let them. This is the right thing to do. The only thing to do, and for the first time in my life I need to grow a pair of balls and stop being such a coward.

It would be easier to just do as my parents want, to marry Rupert and become a billionaire. But since my sister's happiness gave me that glimmer of hope, that seed of possibility, I haven't been able to mindlessly follow orders, to do what my parents say just because they say it.

The moment Dad's fist struck my beautiful, harmless twin, the rose-tinted veil I've been wearing over my eyes for the past four years lifted and I saw myself and my parents for what we truly are. Evil, heartless, power crazed monsters.

"Miss Archibald, it's a pleasure to see you," Mr. Worth says, stepping out from behind his desk the moment I enter the room.

"Hello Mr. Worth, I appreciate you making time to see me," I answer politely, shaking his hand when he offers it.

"Well if you don't mind me saying, you have grown into an absolute vision of beauty, I'm sure your great-grandfather would be immensely proud of you," Mr. Worth gushes.

I smile noncommittally as I think that given how I spent my morning, I'm confident my great-grandfather is turning in his grave in horror.

"Please take a seat, can I get you a drink, coffee, tea, soda?" he offers, circling back behind his desk and lowering himself into his huge leather library chair.

"I'm fine thank you. I'd rather just get straight to business if that's okay?"

His laugh is condescending and indulgent, like I'm an amusing child, and I have to clench my teeth together to stop myself from calling him on his obnoxious behavior.

"Of course, will your parents be joining us?" he asks, his gaze moving to the door as if he expects my parents to enter.

"No, my parents will not be joining us, I'm eighteen now and what I came to discuss has nothing to do with them," I say crisply.

To the lawyer's credit, he straightens in his chair, his body language instantly becoming professional. "Of course. My apologies, how can I be of help."

My hand trembles slightly as I reach into my purse and pull out the envelope containing the doctor's examination report. "Mr. Worth, as I'm sure you're aware, my great-grandfather's will had a lot of clauses and stipulations that I was required to adhere to in order to inherit."

"Yes," he says clearing his throat. "It was an unusual bequest, but those were Harold's wishes."

"I understand," I say patiently. "As my great-grandfather's lawyers and the executors of his will I'm here to make you aware that I am no longer in a position to inherit."

Mr. Worth's eyebrows shoot up so quickly that it's almost comical. "I see," he says, clearing his throat again.

"Here is a letter from my doctor, confirming my ineligibility to inherit," I say, placing the envelope on the desk; watching as he pulls it the rest of the distance toward him, removes the letter, and reads it.

Folding my hands together in my lap, I wait silently as he reads the paperwork that confirms I'm no longer a virgin. I can't look at him, so I scan the wall behind him, staring at the frames that hold degree certificates and other qualifications, until he clears his throat yet again and I'm forced to divert my attention back to him.

"Miss Archibald, are you sure—" he begins.

"Mr. Worth," I say interrupting him. "My great-grandfather's will is the most toxic thing that has ever happened to my family. I'm not entirely sure what his hope was when he wrote it, but I can confidently say that it didn't do what he intended it would. His stipulations didn't make me an honorable person of upstanding moral fortitude like he said it would. All his rules did was destroy my family and make me justify mine and my parents' appalling behavior if it was in line with his wishes and in pursuit of this inheritance."

The older man's eyes widen but I keep speaking, needing him to understand, at least a little, why I'm here.

"If there was the option to walk away from this money I would have taken it, but he forced me into a position where he tied me to this life for another seven years. I'm confident when I say that if I continue to live for the next seven years the way I have been for the last four, there will be nothing redeemable about me left. I want to break this will. I want to be free to try to put my life back together again in some semblance of a way where I can live with myself, and I can't do that until this money is as far away from me as physically possible. That letter is real and I have more proof should I need it, but I'm hoping that I won't."

Mr. Worth's lips are downturned, his expression sad. Lifting his phone from his desk he brings it to his ear, his eyes not leaving mine as he speaks into it. "Could you ask Neville to come to my office please, I need something notarized."

Nine

Sliding the key card into my newly acquired hotel room door lock, I push inside and close the door behind me.

It's done.

It's over.

Dropping my purse to the sofa I fall down after it, my legs giving way as the bravado and adrenaline I've been running on all day starts to dissolve. The cushions are soft and almost warm to the touch beneath me, but I can barely focus on it as my body starts to convulse.

What did I do?

What the hell did I just do?

They'll never forgive me, or maybe they will. Maybe my parents are as disgusted by everything as I have become.

No. That's nothing but wishful thinking, because the truth is what I did today had to happen, but the fall out is going to destroy me, my parents, and maybe even Tallulah too. I just changed all of our lives, the same way that envelope full of papers did all those years ago.

A single tear slides from eyes, rolling down my cheek and falling to my knees. With shaking fingers I touch it, rubbing the moisture between my thumb and forefinger, focusing everything on the simple movement and hoping that it might hold me together.

I made this choice and it was the right one. The first right decision I've made in a really long time. Now I need to wash my face, get dressed, and go to my sister's engagement party. I just hope that she gets at least a few happy moments with her fiancé before everything goes to hell.

———

S moothing the fabric of my dress down, I catch a glimpse of my reflection in the long mirrors that adorn the walls. My dress is black, floor length with cap sleeves, heavily beaded, and clinging to what little curves I have. It's probably more suited to a funeral than a party, but the color black makes me feel powerful and I need all the confidence I can get right now.

The ballroom is full of people as I march through the doorway, eyeing the crowds from left to right searching for Tallulah or Arlo or even one of their friends, Watson, Oliver. Or Carson. But I can't spot them and instead I find my mother. The moment she sees me she pushes her way through the crowd toward me, an expression of pure rage hardening her already cosmetically altered face until she appears to be almost like an angry porcelain doll.

Sighing as silently as I can muster, I school my expression, twisting my lips into an enigmatic smile, the one my mother helped me perfect. It feels almost poetic to be using the skills she helped me perfect against her now, although I doubt she'll see the irony of it.

"Carrigan," she snarls, as her fingers wrap tightly around

my wrist, her nails digging into my skin just hard enough for her to exert some control.

"Mother," I reply cordially. "You look lovely as always."

"Where the hell have you been? What happened last night? The video wasn't there."

Inhaling slowly, I let my eyelids fall shut and try to consider who I'd be now if I'd just ignored them and refused to do all the fucked up things they've had me do since the will was read. Maybe if I had, I'd just be a normal teenager instead of the calculated, conniving bitch I am now.

"Carrigan," Mom hisses, her nails digging further into my skin.

"Do you ever sit back and consider your actions?" I ask quietly.

"What?"

"Do you ever wonder who you'd be, who we'd all be if the money had just been left to grandfather like it should have been."

"What are you talking about? Have you been drinking? Really, it's completely unacceptable for you to put me in this position," Mom chirps, her tone disapproving like I'm inconveniencing her.

"I haven't been drinking mother."

"Then I expect an explanation as to why you did not do as you were told last night?" she demands.

"You mean why didn't I drug and rape my sister's fiancé?" I ask a little too casually.

Her lips curl into a menacing smile and she tips her head slightly to the side. "Dear, how dramatic a description that is. All we're doing is correcting a mistake, Arlo was always intended to be yours and yesterday you should have rectified that problem. Now where is the video?"

"There isn't a video mother," I say with a smirk. I know I

shouldn't be provoking her like this, but I just don't seem to be able to help myself.

"What did you do?" she hisses.

"Do you consider yourself evil?"

Mom's lips part and I think she tries to narrow her eyes at me, but the plastic surgery and Botox stops any real expression from forming.

"Because I do," I tell her, watching her, waiting for some sign of recognition, like somehow she sees how despicable we've become.

She blinks slowly, sighing lightly as her mouth curves back into a smirk. "I'm not evil child, I'm motivated. I'm doing what any mother would do to secure her daughter's future."

I laugh, the sound cold and harsh falling from my lips. "It's over Mother."

"What are you talking about?"

"It's over, it's all over," I say, yanking my arm from her grip and escaping into the crowd of people that are all turning to the stage as my sister and Arlo make their entrance.

Tallulah looks stunning in a deep red gown and Arlo looks as handsome as ever in a classic fitted suit, but it's the way they're looking at each other that makes an ache start in my chest. I'm not entirely sure what's going on between them, I know they're having sex, but until the other day I honestly thought it was all just an act. Looking at them tonight, it's obvious it's not.

Arlo's arm is around her waist, holding her close like he's terrified she might leave and he can't bear to be without her. He keeps looking down at her, like she's the only thing keeping him sane, and that look is filled with more love than I thought it was possible to give another person. But it's not all him, she's smiling too, leaning her back against his chest, knowing that he's there, that he wouldn't let her go. There's a contentment in her expression that I've never seen before.

I've known for years that my sister was nothing like me, but I've never seen it be more evident than it is right now. She's full of light, her smile is only for him and even though she's clinging to his jacket she's not holding him to her or tying him down, she just wants to be close to him because she loves him.

This isn't an intimate moment, it's just an innocent touch between two people who are so in love they can't help but show it to the world. Logically I can recognize the emotion, but it doesn't make any sense to me, I can't understand it. Why does she love him? Why does he love her? How do they know?

I don't think I'm capable of an emotion with as much depth as love, in fact I'm pretty sure I'm not. But if that's true why am I jealous?

"Ladies and gentlemen," Mr. Archibald says, calling everyone's attention as he speaks into a microphone at the front of the stage. "I'm sure you'll all agree that love is a truly wonderful thing. Tonight, is all about celebrating the love between my son and my beautiful soon to be daughter-in-law. Please raise your glasses and join me in congratulating the future Mr. and Mrs. Arlo and Tallulah Lexington."

Taking a champagne flute from a passing waiter, I raise my glass and toast my sister and her not-so-fake fiancé, alongside the other couple of hundred people in the room. The envelope folded inside my clutch suddenly feels heavy and weighted, and I know I've done the right thing. The first right thing in far too long.

"Carrigan, we have not finished talking about your

behavior," my mother says from behind me, her voice laced with barely restrained anger.

Sighing, I spin around to face her, my glass of champagne held aloft in one hand, my clutch with the envelope held tightly in the other. "I agree, we're not finished. But I think this is a family matter, so perhaps, you, Dad, Tallulah, Arlo and I should discuss this together."

Before she has a chance to speak, I down my champagne and deposit the glass on the tray of yet another passing waiter. Reaching for her, I grip her wrist tightly and move, dragging her along with me, my own nails digging into her skin just like she did to me earlier. Weaving in and out of people, I smile politely as I pass, towing my mother behind me until I find my sister, her eyes widening when she spots me.

Arlo's body language instantly changes from happy and soft, to alert and on guard, his arm circles my sister's waist, pulling her to his side and slightly behind him. The move makes me smile and his expression becomes quizzical but guarded.

Stopping when I reach them, I smile sweetly to the older man who is congratulating them, waiting quietly as he makes small talk. He leaves a moment later and Tallulah's gaze turns to me.

"Are you okay?" she asks, not even glancing in our mother's direction.

"I will be."

She nods, but doesn't speak again and we all fall silent.

"Mom, perhaps you could give Dad a call, ask him to come here so we can all have a lovely family chat," I suggest, releasing my grip on her as I turn to the side, placing myself in the middle with my mother to my left and Tallulah and Arlo to my right

No one speaks as my mom pulls out her cell phone and

taps at the screen, lifting it to her ear and asking Dad to come to us.

He appears at her side a moment later. "What's the meaning of this?" he demands, his voice nothing but condemnation as he sneers at my sister.

Inhaling slowly, I swallow down my rising panic and try to compose myself. This is it. This is the moment it all ends, the first truly good thing I've done since that godforsaken will was read.

"Tallulah," I say, my voice cracking a little as I look at my sister. "I got you guys an engagement present."

My twin's lips shake a little and I can see the fear and hope in her eyes. She thinks I can be good, that I'm as much a victim of our parents as she is, but she's wrong. I'm as guilty as they are.

Opening my clutch I slide the envelope free, unfolding it as I pass it to my sister. She reaches out and takes it from me, her hands shaking a little as she does.

"What is it?" Mom demands, stepping forward as if she intends to take the envelope from her.

"Why don't you read it aloud," I suggest.

Tallulah slides the single sheet of notarized paper free and scans the words, her mouth splitting into a wide smile. "This letter certifies that Miss Carrigan Prudence Archibald has failed to meet the stipulations required to meet the terms of the last will and testament of Mr. Harold Archibald the third, and as such relinquishes all claim on the inheritance."

"What?" Mom screeches, ripping the letter from Tallulah's hands and reading, her eyes wide and horrified as the truth of it sinks in.

"It's all real," I say. "You can confirm it with Mr. Worth, I told him to expect your call, but he'll only confirm what that letter says. I am no longer the beneficiary of great-grandfather's will. It's over."

The sound of my mother's open palm connecting with my cheek, combined with her yell of anger, is loud enough to draw the attention of at least twenty people. Enough of them witness her slapping me that within fifteen minutes the entire room will know.

I don't clutch at my face, even though I can feel the sting and heat blooming in my cheek. Instead I enjoy watching the realization dawn in my mother's eyes that not only did she just assault me in a room full of high society, but that the money she wants more than anything else in the world won't ever be hers.

"I think it might be time for you to leave," Arlo says, glaring at my parents as Tallulah rushes to my side, her hand sliding into mine and squeezing lightly.

My dad just shakes his head, the disgust in his eyes as he looks at me and my twin so abhorrent that I can't hold his gaze.

"You stupid, stupid girl," Mom sneers. "The only thing you've ever had going for you was that money. Now you're nothing."

"Goodbye mother," Tallulah says, her voice stronger than I could ever manage.

I don't look up as my parents leave, because as much as I want to hate them, as much as I do hate them, they're all I know. I am who they decided I would be. Everything I am is the person they molded me into and even though I know it was wrong, that they're wrong, I can't help that a part of me wants to run after them, to beg for forgiveness.

"You did it," my sister whispers, awe lacing each word.

Inhaling sharply, I lift my eyes and force a brittle smile

onto my lips. "It's over. Neither of us have anything either of them want anymore."

"Thank you," she gushes, throwing her arms around me and pulling me into a hug, holding me tight.

I freeze, not sure what to do with her affection. I've done nothing to deserve it.

"This is the best day ever," she cries, releasing me to throw herself at Arlo. He catches her, lifting her easily off the ground and spinning her in a circle as she giggles.

"Let's get a drink and celebrate," Arlo says, smiling at me as he lowers Tallulah to the ground, holding her against his chest.

"Yes," Tallulah cries, "Where are the guys? We need cocktails and shots."

"I'll go and find them," I offer, forcing a smile onto my lips and hoping that it looks convincing.

Launching herself from Arlo, she throws her arms around me again, circling my neck, her sweet laugh against my ear. "You did it. Thank you," she says, her voice crackling a little.

"I'm sorry it took me so long," I reply.

Releasing me she turns back into Arlo's arms.

"I'll be right back with the others," I say, turning and blending into the groups of people. Only instead of searching for her friends I make a beeline for the exit and walk straight out, not looking back as I leave the hotel, my sister, and her misplaced thanks behind me.

M y cell beeps again signaling another message, but I
already know who it is without even having to
glance at the screen. Tallulah has been calling and texting me
constantly since I left her and Arlo's engagement party last
night. I sent her one message, letting her know that I was fine,
but apart from that I've been ignoring her.

My sister sees me with rose tinted glasses and I can't
allow her distorted view of me to let myself forget who and
what I really am.

For a second, I consider that the message could be from
one of my parents, but I quickly dismiss the thought and the
tiny pang of hope that comes with it. They won't contact me,
I'm of no use or importance to them now that I've
deliberately sabotaged my inheritance. Without that money
I'm barely even a blip on the radar of their life. Before the
will, Tallulah and I were an afterthought, now I imagine
they'll do their best to forget about us all together.

Glancing around I take in the empty, impersonal hotel
room. I'm alone, and for the first time in years I feel truly
lost. My friends, my life, my entire identity, was all

constructed around the stipulations of the will and without those strict guidelines, now that the expectation is gone, I don't know what to do, and who to be.

My sister wants to help, she wants to support me, but I just can't accept it. Tallulah, or I suppose I should probably start calling her Tally, is my twin, but honestly I find her inane goodness infuriating.

She's a genuinely good person and I have no idea what to do with someone like that. My default setting is superior bitch and I'm not sure even she can change that, or if I actually want her to. I'm good at flirting with the guys I'm told to flirt with and ignoring the ones I'm told are beneath me. I'm good at following the rules. So what the hell am I supposed to do now that the rules don't matter?

Tomorrow I have to go to school, I don't know how fast news that I'm not longer an heiress will take to spread, but I'm sure it won't be long. I have less than six months left at St Augustus but I know the others will smell the blood in the water the moment I walk through the doors, and I won't have the shadow of the money to protect me.

As freshmen, Tally and I were invisible until that money made me a queen, now that it's gone, I'm just like everyone else. I forced my sister to pretend to be me, to ignore her own identity and do my bidding and now everything's coming full circle. My identity is so engrained in that money that I stand a better chance trying to pretend to be my twin, than I do figuring out who I am without the will hanging over my head.

Glancing around me, the beautiful hotel room feels bleak and oppressive, the walls slowly closing in on me as I sit in the same spot I've been in for hours, still wearing my gown from last night. The few tears I've shed have left ugly black streaks down my cheeks and I feel dirty and pathetic.

"You are pathetic," I say aloud, sighing and rolling my eyes at myself.

Pushing myself off the sofa, I struggle to unzip the heavy dress, letting it fall to the floor and stepping over it as I make my way to the bathroom. Twisting the shiny taps, the water gushes out and into the deep tub, steam instantly rising as the hot water steadily fills. Stripping out of my bra and panties I climb in while the water's still running, ignoring the fact that it's too hot and that I can feel my skin burning.

Sitting down, I exhale raggedly as the water rises around me, gradually engulfing my body, the heat intense but strangely cathartic as my limbs slowly become numb and weightless.

Closing my eyes, I let my head fall back to rest against the side of the tub and concentrate on breathing. In and out, in and out. The steam fills my lungs making me feel like I'm eating the air instead of breathing. The water is almost completely covering me now, the heat so intense sweat is beading across my brow, but I don't make any effort to cool it, I just lay there letting it wash away a thin layer of my sins.

As the water continues to rise, I let myself sink further, sliding beneath the surface as heat consumes my face. I open my eyes, staring up at the unfamiliar ceiling above me, distorted by the water as I lay still and unmoving.

All I can hear is the muffled sound of the taps running; of more and more water coming over me, suffocating me, imprisoning me. It's peaceful. I've always loved the sensation of jumping into a pool, that moment when all you can hear is the sound of your own heart.

For a second I wonder what would happen if I just stayed down here, beneath the water where it's warm and quiet. How long would my body allow me to deprive myself of oxygen?

Would I eventually be forced to the surface or would I drown before my brain tried to save me?

Closing my eyes again I revel in the peacefulness of it down here. Allowing a bubble to plume from my mouth, my lungs start to protest, the lack of air noticeable as my chest starts to burn and my body instinctively tries to move me to the surface, fighting against my brain's desire to stay here in the warmth, in the quiet.

Right now I just want to feel the peace, to bask in the silence where nothing matters but the beating of my own heart. I know I don't have long left, that self-preservation will propel me to the surface, to the oxygen I need to survive, but for this moment I'm nothing, and it's blissful.

I don't want to die. I'm not too noble for suicide, I'm simply too cowardly to be able to actually go through with it, and really how cliché would it be for the silly little heiress to kill herself after she deliberately sabotaged her inheritance.

Bursting from the water I gasp, breathing in deep pulls of the balmy steam filled air and filling my lungs with life affirming oxygen. A wry scoff falls from my lips once my lungs have stopped burning and I'm no longer panting for breath. I'm a joke. I feel the weight of my thoughts settle over me as I rest my head against the tub.

I don't even have enough conviction to despise myself, even though I should. The small voice in the back of my mind is still whispering that I did what I had to, that I stopped it before it went too far, that I helped when she needed it. But it was all too little too late.

Soaking for a while longer, my skin has wrinkled and the water has cooled by the time I climb out and wrap myself in a huge fluffy towel. Avoiding the mirror, I pad into the bedroom and sink down onto the bed, not bothering to dry myself, my limbs too lethargic to move.

Eventually I crawl under the covers still wrapped in the towel and let sleep take me, hoping that the shame and disgrace I feel will let me hide in my dreams.

———————

T he sun is peeking through the blinds when I open my eyes. It's morning and I should be getting up and going to school, but I don't move. I can't face the other students, my sister, her fiancé, or their friends, especially not *him*.

Carson Windsor was nothing but a blip on my radar until two days ago. Everything changed the moment I asked him for his help and now he's something to me. He's someone who will forever be entwined with me and I don't want that, but no matter how much I downplay it in my head, I lost my virginity to him and that's not something you can force yourself to forget. I don't want him to be important, to be anything more than my sister's friend, but he is and there's nothing I can do to change that now.

Closing my eyes, I decide to just pretend today doesn't exist. I'll be an adult tomorrow, but for today I want to be a child who gets to hide beneath the comforter, away from real life and the monsters that live there.

She's not here. I think I knew she wouldn't come, but I'm still bothered. I don't like Carrigan, I never have. But what happened, that's not something I can just forget. Maybe it's guilt, or some misplaced sense of comradery, but whatever it is, I can't just pretend like it didn't happen.

I only caught a glimpse of her at the party, barely a passing glance before she was gone with nothing but my friend's elation left in her wake. Priss did it, she broke the will, freed both her and her sister and confronted her parents. Then she just walked away, disappeared. She didn't even wait long enough to celebrate their freedom like Tally wanted her to.

Tally is beside herself, terrified that their parents have Carrigan, that they'll want revenge, but I'm pretty sure Priss is just holed up somewhere licking her wounds. I have her cell number now, it's saved in my contacts, teasing me, but I haven't dialed it or even sent her a text, because I already know she'll ignore me.

Her absence shouldn't affect me. We weren't friends before we fucked, we aren't friends now, but there's something between us that I'm not ready to forget. She's haunting me. My dick gets hard the moment her name is mentioned, and I've lost count of how many times I've watched and re-watched the video of the two of us together since she got into that cab and drove away from me.

I'm not sure if my pride's hurt that she could run out on me without even a backward glance, or if I'm just not done with her yet, but either way, I need to see her and she's not here.

"Where is she?" Tally asks, her eyes wide and full of worry.

"She'll be fine, she's probably just taking a couple of days to get her head around everything that's happened," Arlo tells her, pulling her into him to soothe her.

"What did happen?" Tally asks, turning her attention to me.

"She broke the will," I say casually. The others want to know what I did to help Carrigan, but for some inexplicable reason it feels wrong to tell them that we had sex. I'm pretty sure they all know we did, but unless Priss admits it, I don't plan to confirm it.

"Have you spoken to her?" Tally asks me for the fifth time already this morning.

"If I had, I'd tell you," I assure her, leaning down and pressing a kiss against her cheek before I shoulder my bag and head for my first class with Olly at my side.

"You fucked her, didn't you?" he asks, a grin spread wide across his face.

Forcing a neutral expression onto my face I sigh. "Look the will's broken and the girls are free of it, that's all that matters. Hopefully Carrigan will turn up soon and Tally can stop freaking out."

Olly's grin doesn't lessen as he shakes his head wryly.

"Yeah, yeah, you keep it to yourself. I bet she wasn't such a cold bitch when she was riding your dick."

I swallow down the angry words on my tongue, even though the need to defend Priss burns inside of me. This makes no sense; it was just hot sex, so why am I suddenly team Carrigan? Why am I worried about her, turned on and wanting to fuck her again, consumed by thoughts of her?

Distracted I don't pay attention in class, not that it matters, I could stop turning up altogether and still graduate. One of the joys of being rich, is that you never really have to worry about getting in to your parents alma mata and I received my acceptance letter to Cornel in the post a few weeks ago.

From my seat in the back row I have the perfect view of the entire class, Mr. Harrington has his back to us, writing something on the board, as he excitedly tries to explain some historical event that I can guarantee not a single person in this room gives a fuck about. Unable to resist, I slide my cell from my blazer pocket and open my text app, typing out a message to Carrigan before I can think better of it.

Carson

Where are you Priss?

I stare at the screen for a minute like I can will her to reply, but just like I expected, I get nothing. When the bell rings for lunch I'm really fucking pissed. She was so compliant, so obedient the other day. I told her when I asked her a question I expect her to reply, but now she's ghosting me.

My annoyance only builds during the rest of the day and by the time I'm heading for my Mercedes I'm seething.

"You coming to ours?" Arlo asks, his fingers entwined with Tally's.

"Nah, I've got a video chat with the folks," I say.

Arlo and Tally finally admitted their feelings for each other just before their engagement party and I'm happy for them, but there's only so much of their blissfully in love company I can take. I genuinely love them both, but I'm at the limit of how much PDA I can watch.

Tally's eyes soften a little as she looks at me. "Where are your parents?"

"Dubai I think, I can't really remember, I'm surprised they were here as long as they were this time. They just can't stand staying in one place and Grant is almost as bad."

"You don't want to see Dubai?" she asks, a little wistfully.

"I've been a few times, we have a house there."

"Oh," she says with a giggle. "So you're living in that big house of yours all alone?"

"No, I'm staying on the boat, I hate rattling around the house on my own when they're not here," I say absentmindedly.

"Why don't you just come and stay at Arlo's, it's not like you don't already have your own room there," Tally says, looking to Arlo who just shrugs.

"Bro, you know you're always welcome, you have your key, just move in till your parents get back," Arlo says.

"I'm fine. Staying on The Escape isn't exactly a punishment and Tally honey, you know I adore you, you're like my sister. But you're loud and I can't listen to you scream Arlo's name anymore, I had enough of that when we were all staying there," I say, laughing at her horrified expression.

"Carson," she screams, slapping my arm before she turns and buries her bright red face in Arlo's chest.

"Little Ghost I love it when you scream my name," Arlo laughs, wrapping his arms around her and kissing the top of her head.

"See you guys tomorrow," I say, laughing as I lean down and press a kiss to Tally's cheek before I climb into my car and drive away from school.

The marina is bustling with life by the time I park my car in the lot and I cross the short distance to The Escape, nodding and waving at all the people who greet me. I've stayed here every night since mine and Priss's morning here and I refuse to think about why that is. Her scent is gone, but I still haven't gone home even though I know I should. I should let the cleaning crew erase every trace of her being here, but for some inexplicable reason I just can't.

Priss doesn't owe me anything, we're not a couple, we had one meaningless sexual encounter. So why is it that I'm furious that she dismissed me like I was a barely tolerated employee. Carrigan Archibald is a bitch. She treated her identical twin sister like shit for years, so it really shouldn't come as a surprise that she would do the same to me.

"Thank you for the help."

I can still hear her voice saying the words in my head and anger bursts to life inside of me.

"Thank you for the help."

After what we shared, does she even care how much of a punch in the teeth a thank you and fuck off was?

When I think about Carrigan, all I can see is the way she's hurt Tally, how manipulative she is, how evil. But Priss, the girl I spent the morning with the other day, she's nothing like that, she's quiet and nervous and unsure. Priss was beautiful and passionate and complex. But the problem is that Carrigan and Priss are the same person and I don't know how to accept that. I don't know how to combine the two sides of the single person.

Heading for my bedroom, I strip out of my uniform and pull on a pair of loose basketball shorts before making my way back into the living room and slumping down onto the couch, reaching for the TV remote.

There's homework I should be doing, but I don't care, I want some food, a few beers, and to talk to my parents and brother, but instead I find my fingers reaching for my cell and typing out another text to Priss.

Me – I thought I made myself clear, if I ask you a question I expect you to reply.

I wait for a moment, but she doesn't reply and the urge to hunt her ass down becomes so potent I almost rise from my seat before I remember that she's nothing to me.

It was my condition that it was only once, that we'd have sex once and then it would be done, only now I'm not finished and this isn't over. My cell beeps, pulling me from the edge of irrational rage and I grab it from the couch and lift it up.

Carson

I thought I made myself clear, if I ask you a question I expect you to reply.

My eyes devour her words but instead of consoling me, they only make me angrier.

Priss

I'm just taking some time. I texted Tallulah, she knows I'm okay.

Carson

What the hell are you playing at ignoring
her until now? She was worried.

Priss

I already told you I spoke to her,
she gets it.

My jaw clenches and I have to literally shake my head to escape the unbidden rage that her response has evoked. Before I can stop myself, my fingers are moving across the screen, typing words that I shouldn't be thinking, let alone saying.

Carson

I want to fuck you again.

Hitting send, I throw my cell across the couch hating that I've admitted it, hating that it's true. I don't know if it's my ego that's raising its ugly head because she walked away from me the other morning, or if it's that she was so amenable, doing what I told her to do without question, or maybe it's just that for those few hours she was soft and unsure. I don't know. All I know is that I want more, one more time, a few more hours with her beneath me, while she's mine.

She doesn't reply and I'm not surprised. She's so fucking cold and disassociated that I doubt she felt anything more than the ache between her legs after I took her virginity. Maybe her elusiveness is part of the reason that I want to control her so much, either way I'm a fool for giving her even an ounce of power over me.

Crossing to the kitchen I glance into the empty refrigerator, wishing it was full of food instead of bare except for the remains of last night's take-out. I need to get some groceries, or at least ask our house keeper to do it for me, because I hate living on take-out.

Eyeing my cell like it's a poisonous snake I grab my laptop from my backpack, turn it on and open up a food delivery service, choosing a take-out meal from a nice local restaurant and quickly ordering it.

Frustrated, I cross to the wet bar that's built into the wall of the galley, and always stocked, and pull out a beer. The emptiness of the boat seems to shrink around me and for the first time in a while, I feel lonely. I have places I could be, hell I could take up Arlo and Tally's offer and move in with them, but most of the time I don't mind being alone.

But I can't spend time with Priss's twin tonight. Tally might be my friend, but I can't look at her identical face without thinking of her prickly sister. If Priss's lack of reply has taught me anything it's that me and my dick need to forget all about Carrigan Archibald.

Twelve

Carson

I want to fuck you again.

I've lost count of the amount of times I've read his message, but no matter how many times I close down the app, then reopen it again the words never change. I don't understand. He was the one who said one time only, that was his rule not mine. Not that I ever expected either of us to be interested in a repeat performance, but regardless that was his condition.

He got to be in charge, no condom, and one time only. Those were his rules.

My skin shivers a little as I think about the sound of his voice when he said those things, about the feel of his hands on me, his dick inside of me. It's only been a couple of days but already the pain has faded from the memory, and now all I can see and feel and taste when I think about us together is pleasure. So much pleasure, that now I'm not sure how much of it was real and how much is a fabrication I've created to gloss over the fact that it was just an act and not something deeper.

I know he's expecting a reply, but I have no idea what to say. He hates me. When we had sex it was for a purpose—to break the will—so what reason would we have for doing it again?

Staring desolately at the generic hotel room around me I choke back the sob that threatens to consume me. This morning after I decided not to go to school, everything that's happened in the last few days all hit me at once.

I don't have anywhere to live, my parents hate me, the money is gone and with it everything I envisaged my life would become. My sole purpose for being was getting that money and now I have no idea who I am and what to do.

My trust fund is large enough that I don't have to worry about money, but do I buy a house, an apartment, or do I just stay at this hotel until I graduate and go to college? I'm so used to having my days, my weeks, my life planned out for me, that now all those plans have fallen by the wayside I don't know what to do.

I've picked my cell up, poised to call my mom three times already today, because without her unyielding structure I'm not sure I even know how to exist. For the last few years she's instructed me on everything from my hair and clothes, to my friends and classes. She's organized my life in a series of dinners, events, and parties, and now that none of that matters anymore, my life is just one long empty calendar.

Tallulah would tell me this is my opportunity to discover who I am and figure out what I want to do, but I'm not her. She's brave and I'm weak. If this will has taught us both nothing else it's the fact that when faced with life altering decisions, she will do the right thing and I'll just do as I'm told.

The thought of going back to St Augustus is almost unbearable. By now everyone will know that I'm no longer poised to inherit billions and without it, I'm just a bitch without her pedestal.

There are other prep schools in the city and hundreds across the states, I could enroll somewhere else, where no one knows who I am, where my surname isn't recognized and isn't important. I could finish out my senior year and then go to college. But the reality is that I'm not sure I can get through college without my sister to do the work for me. Apart from a couple of electives, my sister has taken all of my core classes for me for years, she's the smart one, not me.

Tallulah would help me if I asked her to, but isn't that what started all this mess, her coming to my aid because I wasn't smart enough to succeed on my own. No. I've already fucked over my twin enough, this is my problem and I need to grow a pair and figure out how to stand on my own two feet.

Tomorrow I need to go back to school, I'm Carrigan Archibald and if nothing else I know how to act like I'm the smartest person in the room.

It's harder than you'd think to find a prep school uniform at short notice, but there's no way I'm going to collect my clothes from my parents' house. By now they're probably on a beach somewhere avoiding the scandal I caused when I broke the will and my mom attacked me in a room full of high society, but I still don't plan on going back home to find out.

Dressed in the familiar St Augustus uniform I feel a little

more centered than I did yesterday. Out of habit I bought straighteners to do my hair in my custom poker straight style, but this morning something stopped me. Maybe it's my backbone clicking back into place and reminding me who I am. I'm not sure but whatever it is, it pushed me to do something out of character. Staring at my reflection in the mirror, I twist from side to side admiring the halo braid that curves around my head and the loose strands that fall in waves on either side of my face.

Buttoning up my blazer I smooth down the front and glance down at the white socks that cover my knees, reaching almost to my mid-thigh, leaving just an inch or two gap between them and the hem of my skirt that's a little shorter than I'd normally wear it.

I know most people hate the uniform, but I've always loved it. The plaid skirts, the navy blazers, they make me feel like I'm in gossip girl or one of those high school romance films Tallulah loves so much.

For the first time ever I wish I knew how to drive, then I could take myself to school now that I no longer have a driver, but instead I've arranged for a car service to pick me up and deliver me to St Augustus. I'm nervous, but I refuse to show it, so I sling my satchel over my shoulder, stare at myself for a second longer in the mirror, then leave the sanctuary of my hotel room and head downstairs to wait for my car.

I've timed my car to get me to school exactly five minutes before the bell rings. This way I won't be the last person to enter the building, but the majority of the other students will already be at their lockers and hopefully I won't have to deal with the gauntlet of staring faces the moment I get out of the car.

I call on all my years of self-important bravado and etiquette classes to provide me with enough confidence to stride to my locker with my head held high. I won't cower, even though a part of me wants to.

The moment I take my seat in homeroom, Emma Handsworth rushes to my side. "Oh my god Carrigan is it true?" she asks, her eyes wide and horrified. She's the younger sister of one of the guys on my great-grandfather's list, her family is old money, but they were never prestigious enough for my parents to ever let me consider marrying her brother.

"Is what true?" I ask, turning to face her, my expression masked by my all too familiar air of superiority.

"That you're broke?" she shrieks.

I scoff and roll my eyes. "Don't be absurd Emma."

"Fine, not broke, but I mean is it true that the money's gone?"

"The money isn't gone, it still exists, but if what you're asking is, if I'm still in line to inherit it, then the answer is no," I tell her dispassionately.

"What happened?" she asks, taking a physical step back from my desk as if my lack of inheritance could be contagious.

"I'm not sure how that's any of your business," I snap.

"Wow, there's no need to be a bitch," she sneers, looking down her nose at me as she turns and moves back to her desk two rows behind mine.

My eyes fall closed and I pull in a slow reaffirming breath. When I was going to be worth billions I could have told that girl to lick the dirt from my shoes and I'm pretty sure she would have done it just to carry my favor, and now she's calling me a bitch to my face.

If only she knew how awful I truly was, I'm sure she'd be calling me something much worse than that. Her words have confirmed one thing though, everyone knows.

The morning drags, each moment feeling like a thousand, as I ignore all the pointed glances my classmates give me. I can almost feel their thoughts; *How the mighty have fallen.*

Money really is power and without it, I'm just another rich girl in a school full of rich kids. I'm a no one, the bottom of the totem pole and it's only a matter of time until someone decides to remind me of that.

"Carrigan." I hear my sister's voice a moment before she barrels into me, her arms reaching around me as she pulls me in for a hug. I freeze, the physical contact from her unexpected and a little weird. Our family are not huggers, in fact we're not tactile at all. I can probably count on one hand how many times either of my parents has hugged me. But then Tallulah has never been like the rest of us.

When I don't reciprocate her embrace she pulls back, melting into Arlo's arms when he appears behind her. "Are you okay? Where are you staying?" she asks.

"I'm fine, I'm at a hotel for the moment," I tell her stiffly. Even though we've become less hostile toward each other the last month or so, I don't feel comfortable being around her like this, when she's being so nice. I deserve her hate; I want her hate. I have no idea what to do with all this concern she keeps showing me.

"What hotel? Why don't you come and stay with me and Arlo? That's okay isn't it?" she asks her fiancé.

"Of course," he says, looking down at her with so much love I feel a little sick. It's not that I begrudge my sister and Arlo their happiness, it's more that I don't know how to deal with it. I never thought I'd have that. Marriage was always going to be an arrangement for me, so to see them actually fall in love seems odd. "I'm fine, but thank you for the offer," I say, shouldering my bag and turning to leave, not wanting to spend more time than I have to with the happy couple.

"Wait, where are you going?" my sister asks.

"Lunch," I say, not turning to look at her as I continue to walk away.

"Why don't you sit with us?" she says, and I can practically hear the hope in her voice.

If I was a nicer person I'd embrace her olive branch. In fact most people would be overwhelmed by how generous my twin is being toward me, considering my behavior for the last few years. But the truth is that I'm not a nice person. "Look," I say, spinning around to face her. "I know you think I'm just like you, and that now we have this bond or whatever. But nothing's changed Tallulah. We're not friends, all this didn't unite us. I did what I had to do to save myself, and it worked out that it saved you too. So let's not pretend that we're real sisters or that we're going to skip off into the sunset together, because we're not, okay."

I turn to leave and gasp as I almost slam straight into Carson, his brows furrowed together, his eyes hard. Without another word I step past him, my head held high, and make my way into the cafeteria alone, leaving my sister and her new family in my wake.

I've always enjoyed the feel of the envious glances from the other students, knowing they were looking and wishing they were me. But today all I feel is the lack of eyes, no one's looking at me anymore, no one gives a crap about me. Because now I'm the poor relation of Tallulah Archibald, the fiancé of Arlo Lexington, part of the power alliance that will see him, Watson Hilborn, Oliver Montgomery, and Carson

Windsor take the business world by storm when they come of age.

I'm invisible, unimportant, unremarkable, and for the first time since I gave Carson my virginity and broke the will, I regret my decision. I regret walking away from a fortune. I regret ignoring my parents and I regret making myself forgettable again.

Thirteen

Anger bubbles up my throat so hot I can feel it burning as Carrigan brushes past me and walks away. I have to fight the urge not to reach for her and drag her back to me, demand she apologize to her sister, demand she be the girl she was with me, not the harpy we all expect of her.

But right now making sure my friend is okay is more important and so I focus all of my attention on Tally. "Are you okay?" I ask, watching as Arlo pulls her into him, wrapping his arms around her tightly.

"I'm fine. I should have known better than to expect her to have changed because of this. I just sort of hoped she would," she admits quietly.

"She's a bitch," Arlo hisses angrily.

"Maybe the reality of what's happened has hit her now she's back at school," Olly says, but it's pretty obvious he doesn't believe what he's saying.

"Let's go get some lunch, they have the gnocchi you love on today," Arlo coaxes, pressing a kiss to Tally's forehead and leading her toward the lunchroom while the rest of us follow.

I make a point not to look for Carrigan when we enter the cafeteria as a group, I'm angry and if I see her, I'm not sure I'll be able to hold my tongue, so instead I focus on my friends. We sit at the table we always sit at, and Olly places all of our food orders while we chat shit and wait for it to be delivered.

Tally is to my right, her blazer hanging over the back of her seat. My eyes catch on the small inside pocket and before I can stop myself, I'm leaning forward and sliding the old key that's hidden in there free from the fabric and concealing it in my hands.

The first time Arlo saw Tally she was sneaking out of the old disused dark room. She used it as a place to hide from her sister, and the rest of the school when none of us had any idea she even existed.

I haven't really thought about that room since the day I stood guard outside of it, after Arlo proposed to Tally publicly in front of half the school. I don't think she's been inside the room since. Arlo forced her to stop hiding that day and since the first confrontation with her parents, we've made it our mission to make sure everyone at St Augustus knows who she is.

Dropping the key into my pants pocket, I pull my cell out and type a message before I can stop myself.

Carson

We need to talk. Meet me by the lockers in two minutes.

Expecting her to ignore me, I lift my head and scan the room for her, finding her at her usual table, only instead of surrounded by minions like she's always been in the past, she's alone.

I watch her read the text, then turn to look at me, her expression shuttered. Smug satisfaction fills me as I watch her slide her cell into her purse, take a forkful of her food, then push away from the table, grab her stuff, and leave.

"I'll be back in a bit, I forgot something in my car," I say absently, as I rise from the table and slowly leave the room. Priss is stood by our lockers, her posture relaxed and confident like she hasn't got a care in the world.

When I reach her side, I allow my gaze to lock with hers, I let my eyes harden and enjoy the visible swallow she has in reaction. Tipping my head in the direction of the dark room I walk past her, not looking back.

She can't see my smile when I hear her move to follow me, but a sense of power rushes through me at her willingness to still do as I say. It only takes a couple of minutes to reach the door to the dark room and I take the key from my pocket, checking that no one is watching as I unlock the door and gesture for Carrigan to go inside.

Following her in I close and lock the door behind me, only then realizing that I have no idea why I'm here, why I told her I needed to talk to her, or why I wanted her alone in this room with me.

"What?" she snaps after what feels like an eternally long silence.

"You upset your sister."

"Are you serious? You bought me to this dusty, empty room so you could tell me off for upsetting my sister," she hisses, rolling her eyes, annoyance pouring from her in waves.

"You're being a bitch Priss," I snarl, taking a step closer to her. I'm stalling, because I still don't know why I bought her here. All I know is that I wanted to be near her, that I want to touch her.

"So I'm told," she says sardonically, crossing her arms over her chest and popping her hip, her lips pursed together.

"You never replied to my message," I say, closing the distance between us with another step.

Her shoulders tense perceptively and her arms seem to cross a little tighter. For a moment I wonder if she's scared. I've never hurt her, never done anything without her being right there with me, loving it as much as I was.

I watch as her tongue bobs out, coating her lips in shiny wetness. Her mouth is full and pouty but I've never kissed her. It felt too intimate, which is ironic considering I've tasted her pussy. The other morning I never even considered pressing my lips to hers, but right now I'm so tempted. I'm tempted to close the final gap between us and take her mouth, own it like I own the rest of her.

"Why are you doing this?" she whispers.

"What am I doing?" I ask, smiling as I reach out and run the back of my knuckles over the apple of her cheek.

She swallows, trying to turn her face away from my touch but not moving far enough to actually free herself. "It was just sex, to break the will, that's all."

"Did you enjoy it?" I ask, stroking my knuckle down her cheek until I can grip her chin between my thumb and forefinger.

"Carson."

"Did you like the way it felt to have my tongue, my fingers, my cock inside you," I purr seductively, lifting her chin up and forcing her to look right at me.

"I…"

"Did you enjoy giving up control to me and letting me use you. Did you like it when I made you come over and over?"

Her lips part but no words come out. She's not Carrigan

right now, she's not caustic and antagonistic, she's soft and pliant, she's my Priss.

"If you want to leave, then go now, I won't stop you. But if you stay I'm going to touch you. Pick, make a decision right now, you have a minute," I say, dropping my hold on her and taking a step back, leaving her path to the door clear.

Silently I count down, keeping my gaze locked with hers, waiting for her to move. She shuffles on the spot, crossing and uncrossing her arms, but she doesn't leave.

After what feels like a lifetime I move toward her again. "Time's up Priss, if you're staying then turn around, bend over, and hold on to the arm of the couch."

I expect her to bolt for the door, it's one thing to have the bravado to stay put when I've practically taunted her with the orgasms I gave her, but it's another to cede control to me again, to do as I say when there's no reason for this, other than want and need.

She wavers on the spot, her arms falling to her sides, then she slowly turns, moving the few steps to the couch, and bends.

I feel my eyes widen as the hem of her skirt lifts with her movement, not revealing her panties, but giving me the perfect view of the creamy skin on the back of her thighs. Her hands rest on the arm of the couch and she gasps, the sound barely audible, like she's surprised herself.

"Perfect," I whisper.

For a minute I just stare at her, thinking about all the things I want to do to her, with her. Stepping forward I reach her in two strides and slide my palm across her exposed skin. "I never appreciated this uniform until now. Seeing you bent over like this is making me see it in a whole new light. I'm enjoying the naughty little schoolgirl idea. I think you've been bad, don't you Priss?" I taunt, stepping between her legs and forcing her to shuffle her feet further apart.

"Carson," she snaps, impatiently.

"I asked you a question Priss. Do you think you've been bad?"

"No," she spits, glaring up at me as she looks over her shoulder, her gaze imperious even in her submissive, vulnerable position.

Flipping her skirt up, I expose her pale pink satin panties, caressing them with my fingers before I step forward and grind my hard dick against her ass. "I think you've been a bitch Priss. I think since the moment you ran from me with nothing but a fuck you, you've been a bad girl. You've ignored me, you've ignored your sister and I'd lay money on the fact that you've been a bitch to everyone who's spoken to you today."

"Are you going to touch me, or is all this so you can tell me off?" she hisses angrily, but I can hear the lust in her voice even as she tries to hide it.

"Is that what you want? Do you want me to rip these panties off and then fuck you rough and hard? Do you want me to take you, like I hate you?" Bending my knees I grind against her again, feeling her push back into my dick.

"Are you wet for me?" I growl.

"Yes," she rasps, the word sounding like it was torn from her throat.

Sliding my hand between us, I push her panties to the side and thrust one finger deep into her hot, wet cunt. "So fucking tight," I growl, as I pump my finger in and out of her, adding a second finger and stretching her as she pushes back against me, riding my hand.

"Oh god," she sighs, breathlessly.

"I want you to come on my fingers Priss, ride my hand

and make yourself come," I demand, pushing in deeper each time and adding a third finger so her cunt is full and her arousal is coating my hand.

Sliding my other palm around her stomach I find her clit, rubbing and circling as she bounces against my hand. "That's it Priss, come for me."

Her gasps and mewls have me hardening until my dick feels like an iron rod beneath my slacks and then she comes and a gush of liquid rushes down my hand, dripping to her panties and the floor beneath us, making my stomach clench with lust.

Her cunt is still clenching around my fingers when I pull them out of her, dragging her panties off her ass and down her legs and shoving them into my pocket once she's lifted her legs free of them.

"I want to fuck you Priss," I say, leaning over her and biting the back of her neck.

"Yes, god yes, Carson please," she begs, her hips still grinding, her pussy empty but desperate to be filled.

"Bend right over the arm, ass in the air," I order, unbuttoning my pants while she eagerly complies. Grabbing her hips in my hands I slam my dick all the way inside her on one long thrust, loving the sharp gasp of surprise she makes.

I lose myself in her, rolling my hips, filling her deep with every thrust as I fuck her hard from behind, while she moans and gasps and clamps down on my dick like she thinks I'm going stop. As if I could stop. She's taking me just as much as I'm taking her and I couldn't stop now even if I wanted to. I'm a slave to her in this moment, she might think I'm in control, but there's nothing further from the truth, this is her show and I'm just here for the ride.

Unable to reach her clit from this position, I slap her ass hard, loving the sharp hiss of breath she takes. "Play with your clit Priss, I'm close, but you need to come first. Make yourself come," I demand, slamming into her, using my grip on her hips to pull her on and off my dick.

Her arm moves and I watch as she rubs at her clit. Her breaths become more ragged, her movement stalling when I hit that spot inside of her that makes little bursts of, "Oh my god," fall from her lips.

"Fuck, your cunt takes my dick so well Priss, so tight, so fucking perfect. I wish we were filming this too so you could see what I can. So you could watch my cock filling you up, stretching you." As I speak her pussy clamps down on me, until she's crying out, her muscles fluttering, milking my dick making it impossible for me not to follow her. I come with a grunt, slamming into her hard enough to push her forward over the couch, her feet coming off the floor. Once, twice, three times I slam into her with abandon, without finesse and then I still, both of us spent, both breathing hard.

After a minute where neither of us speaks, I pull my dick free, watching as my cum drips from her slit. A fucked up sense of pride fills me as I stare at her well used cunt covered in my release.

Jesus I'm a sick bastard. If she were mine, then maybe it'd be okay to want to fill her cunt with my cum, but she's not mine and this was nothing more than a hot fuck.

Clenching my jaw, I push my dick back into my boxers and rebutton my slacks as I step backwards, giving her enough room to move, even though I really want her to stay there just as she is, spread wide and waiting for round two.

My cell ringing shatters the tension that I can feel thickening with every moment that passes. "You need some help?" I ask, quietly ignoring the call, unable to tear my eyes from her.

"No," she says, her voice small as she pushes upright, her

legs trembling a little. Her gaze drops to the floor and she scans it, searching for something. "Do you see my panties?"

"They're in my pocket," I say, smirking.

Spinning around she holds her hand out expectantly. "Can I have them?"

"No."

"What? Give me my panties."

"No," I say, my smile wide now.

"Carson, give them to me."

"No, I'm keeping them," I tell her, pulling them from my pocket and lifting them to my nose, inhaling deeply. "I can smell you on them, fucking delicious," I say, taunting her.

"I can't spend the rest of the day with no panties on, I'm wearing a skirt," she cries, a hint of bitchiness in her voice.

Closing the distance between us again I snap my hand out and catch her chin between my fingers tightly. "Call it punishment for ignoring me and being a bitch to your sister."

"So us having sex was you punishing me?" she asks incredulously.

"Did it feel like I was punishing you?" I drawl, stroking my thumb over her skin.

"N- no," she stutters.

"You letting me take you again, was you apologizing for leaving the way you did and being a bitch. Your punishment is spending the rest of the day bare, with my cum drying on your cunt, smelling like sex, and remembering that I bent you over and fucked you while you played with yourself.

Her gasp is the sexiest sound I've ever heard and I wait for her to say something, but her eyes stay wide, her lips barely parted with no words breaking free.

"Then when you get back to your hotel later, you can either make a video of you playing with yourself, and send it to me, or you can send me your room number and the address of the hotel you're staying at and I'll come over and finger fuck you till you scream out my name," I whisper, lifting her chin a little, my thumb pulling her bottom lip gently until she parts her lips further, complying with even my unspoken commands, as I push my thumb into her mouth and she sucks.

Her lips pop when I pull my thumb free and release my hold on her. Turning away, I unlock the door and pull the key free, checking the corridor is empty, I push the door open and gesture for her to go through, then I close and lock the door behind us, sliding the key back into my pocket.

Her back is to me and she's cautiously walking away when I call out. "Stop."

Pausing she doesn't turn and I can't help but smile. She might be compliant but she's not meek or weak. When she allows me to be in charge of her and her body, she's giving me that privilege, not just letting me take it.

Moving behind her I press my body into hers, not wrapping my arm around her waist even though I want to. "Talk to you later Priss," I say, leaning down and pressing a soft kiss against the nape of her neck.

My feet are moving, but I'm not sure that I'm the reason they're doing it. The last fifteen minutes definitely happened, I can feel it in the shaking of my legs and the warmth that's still flowing through me after the two orgasms he gave me.

I just had sex with Carson Windsor, again, in a room at our school, over the arm of an old couch. I let him touch me, take me, talk dirty to me, and it was unbelievable. As sense starts to come back to me, I realize that what just happened was so stupid. I need to distance myself from Carson, my sister, and their friends, so why do I seem unable to ignore him?

Everything about him is becoming a compulsion, and even though I know he's bad for me, I can't tell him no. Right now, his cold but exciting commands are the only kind of connection I feel capable of. My sister is there offering me a relationship, but I don't want it, I don't deserve it, but I can't seem to walk away from him as easily as I can her.

Darting into the closest bathroom, I lock myself in a

cubicle and clean up as best as I can without a shower. A part of me feels used, but the rest of me feels like I'm using him just as much and I'm not sure if that makes me pathetic, or a worse person than I thought I was.

After flushing the toilet, I wash my hands then leave the bathroom, stepping into the empty corridor. I used to love coming to St Augustus, this school was my platform, a place where I was adored, even if it was only because they wanted to use me. Now I'm a pariah, the formerly almost super rich, it's not exactly the most impressive title.

As I walk down the corridor, no one looks at me, I don't get more than a cursory wink from a guy who I wouldn't have even glanced at a week ago. I'm not important or interesting anymore, no one envies me, no one wants me, or wants to use me, they just don't care, and as the realization dawns on me, tears fill my eyes.

I want my mom, only she doesn't care now either, because I ruined all of our lives and I have no one else to blame but me. I walk faster, then I'm running down the hallway, through the school and out the front door. I can't be here, I can't be this nobody, I just can't.

Rushing across the lawns I dart for the road, pulling up the Uber app on my cell and almost collapsing with relief when there's a driver only four minutes away from me. My bag is still in my locker, all I have is my cell phone and my credit card that my parents could have cancelled by now, but I can't go back. I can't face my classmate's ambivalence.

When the car pulls to the curb I climb in, wiping the tears from my eyes as I slide into the back seat. The driver glances at me in the rear-view mirror, her hair a mass of black, tightly wound curls that almost touch the roof, and her eyes soften when she sees my tears.

"You okay sweetie?"

I nod, not speaking, and after a moment of awkward silence she pulls away from the curb and blends into the lunchtime traffic. Pulling my cell from my blazer pocket I wonder if maybe Carson will have text me again, but the screen is empty and silent.

When the hotel comes into view, my seatbelt is unclipped and I'm opening the door before we even come to a full stop. "Thanks," I say offhandedly, as I jump free from the car and rush into the hotel lobby. Reaching the elevator I stab the call button, realizing too late that my room key is in my bag, in my locker at school.

Sighing wearily, I turn and pad across the lobby to the reception desk, inhaling sharply and trying to keep the tears that are leaking from my eyes at bay.

"Good afternoon, how may I help you?" the chipper male receptionist asks me, his smile wide, flashing his gleaming white perfectly straight teeth.

"I've lost my key card, could I have a replacement please?" I ask, my voice a little shaky as I try valiantly to keep my emotional meltdown under wraps.

"Of course, what's your room number?"

"1065."

His fingers tap away at the computer in front of him for a second, before he looks up and smiles at me. "Your name please?"

"Carrigan Archibald."

"And do you have the payment card you provided us with?"

Handing over my credit card, I pull in shallow breaths trying to stay calm as misery consumes me.

"Okay, here is your key, we have you due to check out

tomorrow, do you need a wakeup call or any breakfast orders placing?" he asks, his smile never slipping an inch.

"No, I need to extend my stay for a week please," I say, turning to leave, my new key card gripped tightly in my hand.

"Miss Archibald, I apologize, but I'm afraid your room isn't available after tomorrow."

"Okay, just book me into a different suite," I say.

"I'm afraid all of the suites are booked for the next five days, we have a large group of guests that have reserved all of the suites, as well as both penthouse apartments. We do have standard rooms available," he says, his infuriating smile still firmly fixed in place.

"Oh my god, are you serious," I shriek, the tears I've been fighting to hold back finally breaking free.

"Please accept my apologies Miss Archibald, I can check at our sister hotel in Brooklyn."

"No," I snap, waving my hand at him. "Fine, just give me the key to my new room and I'll move now, there's no point waiting until the morning," I cry, looking away, not wanting him to see my composure slip even further.

"Of course," he says, clicking at the keys on the keyboard for a second. "Here is your new key, your room is 459. Call down to reception once you're ready and I can send Henry up to assist you with your luggage if you need, and please feel free to order anything you'd like on room service as an apology for your inconvenience. Can I book you a wakeup call or breakfast?"

"No," I snap, grabbing the key from him and walking away before he has a chance to say another word.

It only takes me a few minutes to collect my handful of possessions from my suite and move them to my new standard room. By the time I'm lying on my bed, staring at the tiny room around me, my tears refuse to stay in anymore and I collapse in a heap of loud uncontrollable sobs.

I'm not sure if I'm crying for the loss of my old life, the money, or the prestige, or if I'm just crying because I've never felt more alone in my life. Whatever the reason I sob until my eyes are gritty and swollen and the pillow beneath my head is wet.

Grabbing my cell, I do what I've been doing for the last four years, I dial my mom's number, knowing that she will tell me what to do. Only instead of the mother who has spent every day for the last few years shaping both me and my life into what she wants, I'm met with a recorded robotic message advising that this number has been disconnected.

I dial my father's number next and receive the same message. My fingers are trembling as I dial the house number and I sag with relief when someone answers.

"Archibald residence."

"Hi could I speak to Vanessa please," I say.

"Who's calling please?"

"It's Carrigan, her daughter."

"Oh," the unfamiliar female voice says. "I'm afraid your parents aren't here, they're out of the country."

"Who are you? Where's Mrs. Humphries?" I demand.

"I'm the new housekeeper, Geraldine. Your parents advised me that they have no immediate plans to return to the house this year," she says, sounding unsure.

"Right, of course," I say, forcing my voice to become polite and calm. "Just to make you aware, I'll be sending a moving firm around in the next few days to collect my belongings."

"Err, I'm afraid, Mr. & Mrs. Archibald have given me strict instructions not to allow anyone access to the house."

Closing my eyes I suck in a slow breath, scoffing lightly. "Of course. That's fine, thank you," I say slowly, then end the call. My parents have gone, they've disconnected their cells and banned me from the house. I can't even go and get my clothes. This is their way of punishing me, because there's nothing they can do about the money, it's gone, but they can do this. They can take my home, my things, I'd lay money on the fact that they've stopped my credit card and that my cell will be disconnected soon too.

I took the future they wanted from them, so now they're taking from me, in the only way they can. I'm not sure why I'm even surprised, I know what they're capable of, because I've been their weapon of choice for years.

Dropping my cell to the comforter beneath me, I squeeze my eyes shut and just lay there, heartbroken, stupid and alone. Eventually I force my lids to open, to sit up and act. I call the lawyers who deal with my trust fund first, and have them arrange for a new credit card to be overnighted to me, then I contact the cell phone company and change my cell onto a new plan in my name. Thirty minutes later, I at least have access to money and a cell phone my parents can't disconnect, even if I only have a handful of clothes and I'm living in a hotel.

Shuffling up the comforter, my skirt ruffles up, my bare ass rubbing along the soft cotton. It takes me a second to remember that I'm not wearing any panties, because they're in Carson's pocket. I should have insisted he give them back, told him he couldn't keep them, but I was too drunk on orgasms to care.

I only have a couple of pairs of underwear anyway and now I have one less, because he decided to punish me for being a bitch. The though heats my cheeks and my sex clenches, reminding me that he took me unapologetically, fucking me hard and making me come over and over.

Ignoring the thrill that rushes through me, I try to focus on something else. I need to get some clothes, only the thought of going shopping is horrifying, because for the last four years my mom has chosen all my outfits. I trusted her to do it, just like I trusted her to shape my actions and my behavior.

Stripping out of my uniform I slide the hotel robe on, then shove my uniform in the bag for cleaning and place it outside the door. Turning on the shower I hang the robe on the hook on the back of the door and step under the stream of water, using the complimentary shampoo and wishing I had my stuff from home.

Melancholy and anger war with each other as I wash quickly then turn off the shower and dry myself with the white hotel towels. My parents are assholes, but I'm still their daughter and they turned their back on me the moment I stopped doing exactly what they wanted me to do, even though what they wanted me to do was awful and a felony.

Clean and dry I shove my arms into the robe, wrap it around my naked body, and sit back down on the bed. Grabbing the remote I turn on the TV just for some noise to fill the empty room that somehow feels quieter, even though it's a quarter of the size of the suite I've been staying in until now.

My cell beeps and I grab for it, hopeful that maybe it's my mom, that the new housekeeper told her I'd called and that she was reaching out to me, but of course it's not her.

My disappointment dissolves when I see it's a message from Carson.

Carson

Why aren't you in class?

For a minute I think about not replying, then I realize that he's literally the only person I want to talk to, even though I know I shouldn't. I don't understand his agenda anymore, the will is broken, my sister is free, but he's still playing with me. He doesn't seem to want anything from me except my compliance and my body, he doesn't care that I gave away a fortune, he doesn't expect me to be nice.

Carrigan

I had a headache so I left.

Crawling beneath the covers of the bed I roll to my side, place my palm beneath my cheek and close my eyes. My cell beeps again and I sigh. I want to talk to him, but I don't at the same time. He belongs to my sister, he's her friend so I should stay away, but even despite my own warning I click in to see what he text.

Carson

What hotel are you at?

Carrigan

The Haywood.

Carson

Room number?

Carrigan

I'm not up for visitors.

Carson

Room number?

I don't know why I'm stalling, I'm going to tell him, I always was, even though I know I shouldn't.

Carrigan

I wait for his reply, but it doesn't come. Refusing to admit how disappointed I am, I close my eyes and fall asleep, ready for today to be over.

Fifteen

I fully plan to go back to the boat to do my homework, then meet the guys at some charity event we RSVP'd for, back when we were still trying to make sure everyone important knew Tally wasn't her sister. Only instead of going to the marina, I find myself handing my keys to the valet outside the Haywood Hotel.

Riding the elevator to the fourth floor I try not to think too hard about why I'm here. I already fucked her once today and her text said she was sick and not up for visitors, so why am I here instead of with my friends?

Honestly I don't know. Maybe it's because even though she's a bitch, I sort of get it. I mean her parents are fucking awful and yeah Carrigan isn't blameless, but when it counted, she did the right thing. Sometimes, I can almost believe there's something good beneath the awful person she is, something more.

The elevator dings, heralding my arrival on her floor and I stride purposefully toward room 459, rapping my fist against the wooden door when I reach it. I knock again when she doesn't answer. "Priss, open up."

After a minute the door cracks and a rumpled looking Priss appears, peering around the gap. "Carson?"

"Yeah," I say gruffly, pushing the door open and letting myself inside. The room is small, just a normal hotel room and nothing at all like I would have expected her to pick. Weirdly, Tally stayed in a similar room when she fled from her parent's house too. "No suite?"

"Someone rented all the suites and the penthouses," she says derisively with an annoyed shake of her head.

Closing the door behind me a smile spreads across my lips. Just when I'm assuming her and Tally are more similar than either of them realize, she shows me how different they are. She's only wearing a white robe, her hair's messy and her face is fresh and makeup free. She looks perfectly fuckable and my dick rises enthusiastically.

"What are you doing here Carson?" she asks, climbing back into the bed and pulling the covers up over her legs.

"I have no fucking clue," I admit, lowering myself down onto the bed next to her, kicking my shoes off as I stretch out on top of the comforter.

For a second we just sit in strained silence, the rustling of the sheets as Priss fidgets is the only noise.

When she sighs, I turn and look at her, smiling at her consternated expression.

"Do you even like me?" she asks.

"Not particularly. Do you like me?"

"Not really," she says, a faint smile ghosting across her lips.

"You okay?" I ask, shocking myself that I actually care.

"No. But that's my problem, not yours."

I don't know why I do it, but I pull her into me, wrapping my arms around her while she rests her head on my chest. She doesn't fight me, and although I'm sure she'd deny it if I asked, I swear I can feel the wetness of her tears on my shirt.

"I'll order us room service," I say after a while, carefully moving from beneath her and reaching for the phone. "Hi, can I get a bacon cheese burger, a chicken alfredo and two chocolate brownies with whipped cream please." I say, then glance at Priss, "What do you want to drink?"

"A sparkling water please," she says, her eyes a little wide.

"And a sparkling water and a beer please, whatever you have on draft. Thanks." Placing the phone back onto the receiver I turn to look at her and smile.

"I can't eat any of that," she says, her voice laced with annoyance.

"Sure you can."

"I'll get fat."

"Priss, you're skin and bone, who the fuck told you that you'd get fat."

"Everyone in modern society," she says sardonically, flopping back against the pillows.

"And your fuckwit parents I'd guess. Seriously did you listen to everything they told you and just accept it as truth? You're eighteen, it's time to start thinking for yourself," I snarl, frustrated that she's so blinkered by their opinions.

"Fine, yes okay, they told me I'd get fat. My parents told me that I had to do things a certain way, so that's what I did. That doesn't make me an idiot, or maybe it does, but my life was a bit more complicated than most eighteen-year-olds," she says, jumping up and putting the bed between us, her chest heaving up and down. "All I've thought about since the day I got that stupid letter from my great-grandfather is how I was going to make sure I got that money. All I've talked about is who I was going to marry. All I've lived and breathed is those godforsaken rules, so I'm sorry that you think I'm naive or stupid or whatever, maybe I am. But the only thing I've ever done that made me interesting and worthy and loved was having my name written into that will."

As she shouts at me, the front of her robe slips open a little, revealing the swell of her small, pert breasts as her chest lurches up and down. Her hair's wild, her eyes red and wide, and her lips are parted and full. She's a fucking mess, but she's never looked more perfect to me than she does in this moment.

Carrigan is a beautiful woman all the time, she's stunning in a school uniform, in her usual tight dresses and adorned in evening wear. But right now, raw, unkempt and angry, she is fucking glorious.

Moving, I close the distance between us, until I'm pressed up against her, my chest touching hers. She tips her head back to look at me and her eyes tell me that she's just as confused about this as I am.

"This, you in this exact moment, is why I'm here Priss. I don't understand it, but even while I hate you, I need to save you." Closing the distance between us I kiss her, taking her lips and owning her as I slide my tongue into her mouth. I feel her silent moan as she parts her lips, her movements slow and uncertain, as her fingers clutch at the back of my neck, holding me to her, letting me know that she wants this as much as I do.

After a second we find our rhythm. The kiss becomes a game of give and take, as I nip at her full lower lip, turning my head to the side to deepen the kiss. She melts against me, her nipples pressing against my shirt as I hold her to me, pressing her as close as two people can get while fully dressed.

This kiss doesn't feel like a prelude to sex, it's not the

tease that will lead to more. I don't really know what it is, but in this moment with Priss in my arms, hate doesn't matter, who she is doesn't matter, my prejudice and her behavior doesn't matter.

Tally once told me that who you are in the quiet moments is the real you, and right now in the silence of this hotel room, Carrigan Archibald, *my Priss,* is mine and that's all that matters.

Sixteen

This is my first kiss.

That's the thought that's playing on a loop in my head. This is my first kiss, the first time a boy, or anyone, has pressed his lips to mine and it's with Carson Windsor.

The inner teenage girl who dreamed of boys and kisses and love is bouncing around inside of me like a cheerleader on game day. But the cynical, disillusioned eighteen-year-old is warning me that those things aren't in the cards for me, even without the will's obligations hanging over my head.

At first, it's weird. I don't know what to do, how to move, but then my natural instincts kick in and suddenly our lips are in sync. His teeth find my lower lip and bite down. I shouldn't like it but I do, moaning against his mouth as my entire body melts into him, like he's the only reason I'm upright.

Other girls would probably act nonchalant, this is only a kiss, and Carson and I have been in much more explicit situations. But for me, this kiss is the most intimate thing I've ever experienced.

Carson and I are enemies, or we were. I'm not sure whose

side I'm on anymore or even where the lines are drawn, but regardless we aren't allies. I'm clinging to his neck and for right now I don't care who's side he's on, or what war we're engaged in, I just want more.

He's kissing me in spite of who he is, in spite of who I am, or what our circumstances are. He's kissing me because he wants to and I'm kissing him because I just don't seem to be able to help myself.

My eyes are tightly closed, and with his arm banded around my back, half holding me to him, half holding me up, it feels like nothing else in the world exists. All I can smell is his clean, fresh cotton scent, all I can hear are the sounds of my own gasps and moans.

Heat is pooling in my stomach but I don't want this to become sex. Sex with him is impersonal, distant. A wonderful but disassociated act that I've enjoyed on both occasions, but that I never associated with any feeling deeper than lust. This kiss is more, or at least it feels like more. Maybe I just want it to be more.

As quickly as it started the kiss is over and Carson releases me, looking at me strangely for a second before turning and leaving.

Slumping down onto the bed I exhale, confused and frustrated and needy. For him. I'm needy for him. For his touch, for his kisses, for the way when he's around I don't feel like the worst person in the world.

A sharp rap at the door has me jumping up from the bed and darting across the room, my heart leaping excitedly in my chest, hopeful that it's him. That he came back. To me. Fumbling with the handle I open the door, my lips parted, ready to smile, only it's not Carson, it's room service, the wheeled cart piled with silver lidded plates. The food that he ordered, that I can't eat.

A weight settles on my chest, right over the spot where my heart is, but I refuse to allow it to be my heart that's hurting. On autopilot I allow the server to come into the room and arrange the food onto the dressing table, the only available surface in this box of a room. Signing the bill, I add a tip and then close the door behind him as he leaves.

Staring at the plates of food that Carson ordered, I have the sudden urge to fling them across the room. He left, he just left. I shouldn't care, but I do. This boy was my first kiss, my first touch, my first everything. I don't know if he took or I gave, it doesn't really matter either way. But standing here alone, staring at the food he ordered us, I realize that I do care and I have no idea what to do with that.

The beep of my cell phone frees me from my unwanted moment of realization. I've been frozen to the spot, and now my body is freed and I slowly reach for my phone.

Carson

Eat.

A hysterical gurgle of laughter bursts from my throat and I'm typing with one hand as I clap the other across my mouth to stifle the sound.

Carrigan

I DON'T EAT ANY OF THESE FOODS.

Carson

You do now. EAT!!!

I know I should ignore him. He left, and even if he'd stayed he has no right to tell me what to do. Except when we're having sex, and really I shouldn't even let him do it then. Although I am clueless and it's incredibly hot when he uses his growly authoritarian voice.

The smell of food fills the room and I tiptoe cautiously over to the trays. Despite my parents not even being in the country and the fact that they've abandoned me—now I'm no longer of any use to them—I still don't seem to be able to rebel against their rules.

My cell beeps again and I grab for it, using it as an excuse to step away from the delicious smelling food.

Carson

Priss EAT THE GODDAMN FOOD. Send me a picture of you eating and for every plate you empty I'll give you an orgasm.

Dropping my cell to the bed, my lips part and I fight the need to do what he tells me. My resolve lasts only seconds and I edge closer to the food, lifting the lid on one of the plates and inhaling deeply when the scent of rich garlic fills my nose.

Pasta. It's been years since I've been allowed near anything that smelt this good and the creamy pasta looks delicious. Grabbing a fork, I carefully spear a piece of pasta, glancing over my shoulder like I'm expecting my mom to jump out of the closet and yell at me.

The cream hits my tongue and I groan with pleasure. Before I can stop myself, I'm smiling and eating and internally waving my middle finger at my parents and their rules, and it feels good. It feels more than good to defy them, it feels amazing. That's the reason that I eat half the pasta, and it's defiance that drives me to take a bite of the huge burger, licking the oil from my lips as the cheese and beef melt against my tongue.

Lifting the lid on one of the dessert plates, I groan as I stare at the decadent chocolaty brownie and thick fluffy whipped cream. My mom would lose her mind if she thought I was even breathing the same air as this many calories, and I think that might be what pushes me to dig my spoon into it and lift it to my lips. After the first mouthful, all thoughts of rules and parents disappear and its pure want that has me finishing the cake and licking the spoon.

As much as I want to, I don't send a picture of my empty dessert plate to Carson, because he's just like the brownie I gorged on. He's bad for me and even though when he's touching me I love it, ultimately I have to learn to say no.

W hen the car service pulls to a stop at the curb outside the hotel the next morning I sigh, wishing that I'd just stayed in bed, but knowing that I can't keep missing school if I want to actually graduate this year. Because of Tallulah pretty much taking all my classes until a month ago, my GPA is perfect, but I still have to maintain reasonable attendance to be able to graduate.

I don't bother trying to time my arrival to avoid people today, yesterday made it pretty clear that the news of my newly disinherited state has spread like wildfire, so there's no point trying to hide from it.

Climbing out when the driver opens the door I inhale a long slow breath, fortifying myself for the day ahead. I don't want to be here, but I have nowhere else to go either.

Sick of my own self-indulgent thoughts I lift my head up and stride purposefully into the school, smiling sweetly at anyone who stares at me as I walk past. It's time to remember that I'm not some pathetic little girl who needs to be protected. I owned these halls until I gave it up to save me and my sister from a future ruled by money and greed. I need to stop cowering and remember who I am.

Bolstered by my internal pep talk, my stride becomes more purposeful, and I make it to my locker without anyone else looking at me.

"Carrigan," my sister calls, rushing toward me.

Sighing, I open my locker and pull my purse free before turning to face her. As usual now, she's not alone. Arlo is at her heel with Olly, Watson, and Carson all circling around her like her security detail.

Not bothering to speak, I rest my back against my locker and wait for her to say whatever it is she wants to say. My sister is nothing if not tenacious in her pursuit of a relationship with me.

"Have you heard from Mom and Dad?" she asks after a second.

"The last time I spoke to either of them was at your engagement party when I gave you your gift. Both of their cell phone numbers have been disconnected and according to their new housekeeper they're out of the country," I say, trying to hide my hurt.

Tallulah jolts back, clearly shocked and I try not to hate her when the guys all close in around her like they want to share her pain.

"They just left," she says, and I can hear the slight catch in her voice.

Sighing, I nod. "They just left."

She nods, like the physical action is helping her process.

"I need to get to class," I say, unable to hold her eyes now that they're filled with hurt.

"So are you going to move back home now?"

A wry humorless laugh falls from my lips. "The new

housekeeper informed me that our beloved parents have left strict instructions that no one is allowed onto the grounds without their permission. So no, I won't be moving *home*," I say spitting the word like it's poison.

"But what about all your things?" Watson asks, shocking me with how genuinely concerned he looks.

Shrugging I look away, not wanting to see even more pity on their faces.

"You can't even get your stuff? Your clothes and shit?" Carson asks.

"I haven't tried, but as I was basically told I'm not allowed on the premises, I'm going to hazard a guess at no. It doesn't matter."

"Of course it matters," Tallulah cries, reaching for me.

Leaning back I avoid her touch, ignoring the hurt that flashes across her face.

"I'm fine. I'll be fine," I growl, taking another step back, before I spin on the spot and walk away leaving my sister and *her* boys behind me.

The rest of the day only gets worse as I have math, chemistry, and geometry. Taking classes without my sister's help and my parents' bribery is awful. The teachers seem to be deliberately calling on me, like it's my fault my parents stopped paying them to give me A's.

By the time I crawl back into my hotel bed, my school uniform outside my door for cleaning again, I'm exhausted both mentally and physically. My new credit card was waiting for me this morning, so there's nothing stopping me from going to buy the things I need, but I just don't seem to be able to find the energy.

Somewhere deep inside me, I know I'm more resilient than this, that I'm more than capable of looking after myself and coping with my parent's absence, hell Tallulah and I did it for the majority of our lives. But right now, all I feel is raw and exposed.

For so long the money has shielded me from everything except its pursuit. All I had to do was play by the rules and my future was set. I was okay with that, resigned to do what I *had* to do to get that inheritance, and I hate that now that the money's gone I have to feel the consequences of my actions.

My parents get to run away, but I'm still here and now I have to try and learn to live with all the things I've done.

Tallulah thinks that the way I treated her is the worst thing I've done, but she couldn't be any further from the truth. I've manipulated, flirted, and lied over and over again and the only guy who didn't lap it up, is ironically the one who fell in love with my twin.

A sharp rapping at the door makes a prickle of awareness course through me. It's Carson. Apart from the staff, he's the only other person who knows I'm here. But even if there was someone else it could be, I'd still know it was him. Maybe it's that my body remembers what it feels like to be around him and has perked up with his proximity. Whatever it is, I'm off the bed and pulling open the door, because even if I don't really understand it, I want him here.

Seventeen

CARSON

EST 1917

ST AUGUSTUS PREPARATORY SCHOOL

C arrigan Archibald is always walking away from me and I fucking hate it. I know she's not who her sister wants her to be, but they could have a relationship if Priss just stopped being such a prickly bitch. Both of the girls are a product of their fucked up upbringing, but where Tally came out swinging, Carrigan seems to be crumbling.

Her parents have banned her from getting into the house. They know she hasn't got any of her things and they're deliberately stopping her from going home, it wouldn't surprise me to find that her stuff was gone even if she could go back. They're punishing her.

They're supposed to be the adults, the care givers, but those people have never thought of their daughters as anything but a commodity to be used for whatever purpose suits them best.

If she was anyone else I'd feel bad for her, but I'm almost glad that Carrigan's family has done this to her. Its forcing her to see who they really are. They've cut her off from everything familiar and tied to the messed-up existence she's been living in since that godforsaken will came to life and destroyed them.

The need to comfort her, to take care of her is almost blinding, but then I remember who she is and what she's done. No matter how I try, I can't reconcile Carrigan with my Priss, because when I'm near her, I forget all her sins and all I see is the sweet broken girl who needs me.

Watching her in class, all I could think about was how she feels beneath me, the taste of her lips when I kissed her, the way she gave herself over to me in a way no one has ever done before. She's perfect in all the very worst ways, because her perfection blinds me to who she really is.

Lifting my fist to knock at her hotel door again, it swings opens and a tired looking Priss appears in the gap. I don't know why I'm here, but as much as I tried to fight it, I just couldn't stay away. My eyes rake over the white cotton hotel robe and my dick twitches, because I know she's naked beneath it, but I don't think I'm here to fuck her.

Last night I kissed her. I shouldn't have, but she just looked so fucking lost and so fucking sweet and I couldn't resist. But now her mouth is all I can think about. I want her. My body craves her like I've never craved anything else before. Only I ache for more than just her body beneath mine, I want *her* too.

I don't like her, but I want her.

Some weird, fucked up part of me wants to help her, to protect her, to take care of her and I swear I barely even recognize the feeling, because I've never known anyone, not even my family or Tally, that has made me feel this way.

It's unhealthy as fuck. Last night after the stupid fucking charity event, I spent an hour googling all these messed up feelings I have. I'm either about to die from a brain tumor or I like her.

I like Carrigan Archibald.

No. I like Priss. I like the sweet, sad, lonely girl who gave me her body, gave me the right to touch her.

I have control issues. I like things a certain way. But those things are all about me. The guys know about my quirks, but I've never felt compelled to push my oddities onto them.

But I'm itching with the urge to take control of Priss and not just while I fuck her, not just while she's offering her body to me, but I want to take control of her completely. I want to throw her over my shoulder and take her back to The Escape. I want to feed her, buy things for her, be hers.

Shit. I sound like a fucking weirdo even inside my own head. I should be running away from this girl but here I am at her door. Again.

Stepping past her I walk into her room without an invitation.

"Come on in," she says sarcastically, but she doesn't ask me to leave. I wouldn't anyway, I couldn't walk away if I tried.

Crossing to the closet I throw open the door. It's empty except for the dress she wore to the party and the clothes we picked together. Pulling the draws open I find all but one empty, and except for a handful of underwear she literally has nothing.

"Why haven't you been shopping?" I demand.

She shrugs and the robe falls open a little exposing her shoulder.

"I asked you a question," I growl, unreasonably angry at her, at her parents, at myself for not considering that she hadn't been home.

"I'll get round to it," she says, her tone becoming obstinate.

"Get dressed."

"No," she snaps, righting her robe and crossing her arms across her chest.

"Priss I'm not fucking around, get dressed," I say, fighting back the need to yell at her to do as I say.

"No. I'm tired and I don't want to go anywhere."

"Look you can either get dressed and walk with me, or you can be a pain in the ass and I'll carry you out of here in nothing but that robe. Right now I don't give a fuck which option you pick, but either way you're coming with me. You have one minute to make a decision."

Rolling her eyes, she shakes her head dismissively. "Go away Carson. I think we can both agree the sex was great, but we need to stay away from each other, I need to stay away from all of you," she says, sitting down on the edge of the bed and reaching for the TV remote.

"Time's up," I say, fighting back a smirk. She thinks she can send me packing with a bitchy look, she's got no fucking clue how wrong she is.

"Bye Carson," she says, wiggling her fingers at me in a fuck you wave.

A soft laugh falls from my lips as I close the distance between us in a single stride, grab her around the waist, and haul her into the air and over my shoulder.

"Put me down," she screams, beating her fists against my back.

"I gave you a choice Priss, it's not my fault you picked the wrong option. You better hope there's not too many people in reception, because I'm pretty sure you can see your ass out the bottom of this robe," I laugh, ignoring her protests as I grab her cell and room key, open the door, and carry her out.

Shrieking, she writhes around trying to break free of my

hold, but I just laugh and hold her a little tighter. "I gave you a choice Priss."

"Where are you taking me? Put me down Carson, I hate you so much."

"You don't hate me and I don't hate you," I say. Muttering, "That's the fucking problem," beneath my breath.

"Put me down and I'll go and get dressed," she begs.

"It's too late to do as you're told now baby. I asked you do something and you didn't. I'm a man of my word Priss. Haven't I always done what I told you I would?"

"Carson," she cajoles, using the voice I've heard her use on guys before.

"Don't try that bullshit with me Carrigan. I'm not one of those spineless fuckers that will let you do as you please while they wait around begging for scraps, not giving a fuck about anything except the money. I've had you. I've fucking got you, no money, no power, nothing."

"Shut up," she hisses, her voice wavering a little.

Stopping, I lower her to the floor, keeping my arm tightly wrapped around her. "No, you listen. I had you knowing that you didn't come with the extras. Because I couldn't give a fuck about that inheritance."

Slamming my lips against hers, I kiss her with every bit of frustration I can't explain, filling her mouth with my tongue, branding her lips with mine. When her body melts against me I pull away, cupping her cheek and locking my gaze with hers. "I'm not a man you can play with Priss and I promise not to play with you either. All I expect is for you to be you, this you. I don't know what the hell I'm doing, I just know I'm not ready stop.

Picking her up I throw her back over my shoulder again and this time she doesn't fight me. No one says a word as I carry her through the lobby in nothing but a hotel robe. I swear the guy behind the reception desk even smirks as I pass, striding confidently outside and to the valet desk. A few minutes later my car appears and I lower her into the passenger seat before climbing into the driver's seat.

"Where are we going?" she asks, the bitchiness gone from her voice.

"To get you some clothes," I answer, pulling my cell from my pocket and dialing the familiar number, before lifting it to my ear. "Hey," I say when the call connects. "I need a favor." I listen for a moment. "I need a new wardrobe." I can hear Priss's indignant huff but I ignore her. "Size two, okay, see you soon. Thanks bye."

"Who was that?" she demands, turning in her seat to look at me.

"A friend," I say, quickly snapping a picture of her, smiling at her annoyed expression before I ease away from the hotel and into the evening traffic.

"Carson," she whines, when I ignore her and focus on driving.

"Carrigan," I say back, smiling widely.

"Why do you say my name like you're using it as an insult?" she asks.

"Because I prefer Priss," I say simply.

"I don't understand."

"When you're acting like you think Carrigan Archibald ought to act, I call you Carrigan. When you're acting like the girl who gave me her virginity, the one I want to be around, the one I can't keep away from, I call you Priss."

I expect a bitchy response, but instead she stays quiet, not speaking until we pull into the parking lot at the marina.

"I thought we were getting clothes?" she asks.

"We are, after we eat," I tell her, pulling into my usual space and killing the engine. By the time I climb out she already has her door open, eyeing the gravel parking lot warily. "Come here," I say, loving that she doesn't try to fight me as I scoop her into my arms and lift her from the car, closing the door, and then carrying her up onto the deck of The Escape.

She obediently follows me, after I lower her to the floor and open the door to the galley, leaving it wide as I step inside and turn on the lights. Crossing to the refrigerator I pull out a beer for myself and start to grab the ingredients for dinner. "Do you want a beer?" I ask her.

"No thank you," she says quietly.

Straightening I turn to look for her and find her standing cautiously in the doorway. "What's the matter?"

"Nothing," she says, stepping inside, her arms wrapped tightly around herself.

"Priss, why don't you go take a shower, I'll lay out a shirt for you."

For a second I think she's going to argue, but instead she lifts a hand to her hair, smoothing down the back uncomfortably.

Sighing I close the distance between us, curling my arm around her back and pulling her into me. "Baby, if you want to you can stay wearing nothing but this robe for the rest of the night. Fuck, I'd be happier if you took it off and stayed naked all night. I think you're fucking stunning when you're hot and sweaty beneath me. I think you're beautiful mussed and sleepy. My dick has been rock hard for you since the moment you opened that hotel door, because you don't look like Carrigan right now, you look like my Priss, and that is so fucking sexy I am barely keeping my hands to myself," I whisper against her lips, a moment before I kiss her, pressing my rock hard dick against her stomach as I hold her to me.

Her lips are soft and sweet against mine and for a moment

she just lets me kiss her, before she tentatively moves against me, her hands sliding up my chest and around my neck, her tongue tangling with mine. Lifting her off the ground, I groan when her legs automatically wrap around my waist. "I want you," I say, pausing our kiss long enough for the words to fall from my tongue.

"Yes," she gasps, kissing me again, her fingers clinging to me.

Carrying her to the bedroom, I lose myself in the girl in my arms, the enigma that is both bad and good, soft and hard, sweet and toxic. But while I touch her, while she moans and sighs and cries out, she's all Priss, all the girl that I don't seem to be able to escape, the one I think I want to keep.

———

"Come take a shower with me," I whisper against her neck, her naked, damp body pressed against mine.

Without opening her eyes she shakes her head, too drunk on orgasms to move.

Laughing lightly, I untangle myself from her, tapping her ass as I climb out of bed and head for the shower, hoping she'll join me. I turn on the water and immediately step under the stream, not waiting for it to heat up. My dick was in her five minutes ago, but I already want more and if I don't calm down I know I'll go back in there and lose myself between her legs again.

I'm reluctant to wash her scent from my skin, but I push past the feeling and reach for my body wash. When I step out of the bathroom a few minutes later I glance at my bed, anger instantly consuming me when I find it empty.

"Priss," I snarl, stomping into the galley and stopping

short when I spot her drinking from a glass in the kitchen, her nakedness covered by my shirt.

"What's the matter?" she asks, her eyes still soft, wide and innocent.

Relief bursts from me. She's still here and she's still Priss, the cold Carrigan mask nowhere in sight. "Nothing, come here," I order, my voice gruff.

Padding on bare feet she closes the distance between us, pausing a step away from me. "All the way here," I say, crooking a finger and beckoning her forward, a smile spreading across my lips.

Swallowing she sways on her feet. "Carson," she says, an argument obvious on her tongue.

"Priss, I've got no idea what we're doing, why I can't leave you alone, but I can't and I don't want to. So come here and kiss me, because I think you want me just as much as I want you. Maybe we don't need to understand it, and we can just enjoy it instead."

Her white teeth emerge and she worries her bottom lip. For a moment I think she's going to run, but instead she takes the step and wraps herself around me.

A knock at the window startles us both and she tries to pull away as I hold her close. Looking up I smile at the familiar face. "Hey, come on in," I say.

Loosening my hold on Priss, she turns to look at our guest and I watch as his face pales.

"Tally," Fitzy gasps.

"No," I cry as I feel Priss go rigid in my arms. "No, Fitzy, this is Carrigan."

S lowly I turn to fully face the man who just walking in, his expression horrified at first, then shocked.

"Oh my god," he says, his eyes wide as he takes me in. "You really are identical, but not at the same time."

"Carrigan this is Fitzwilliam Van De Burg," Carson Says. "Fitzy, this is Carrigan Archibald."

"Well it is lovely to meet you," the man says, walking forward, his hand held out for me to shake.

I take it and he squeezes lightly, almost affectionately which is surprising. "It's nice to meet you Mr. Van De Burg."

"Oh please call me Fitzy," he says jovially, before looking up at Carson and scowling. "Why didn't you tell me it was Tally's sister?"

"I can't believe you thought I'd be hugging Tally while I was naked," Carson says with a laugh.

"Well," Fitzy says, clearing his throat.

My eyes widen as I remember that I'm only wearing Carson's shirt. Oh my god, Carson is naked and I'm just in his shirt. My hair a bird's nest and it literally couldn't be any more obvious that we just had sex. "I should go," I say, refusing to look at anything but the floor as I point roughly in the direction of the bedroom.

"Go shower and I'll make dinner," Carson says, pulling me to him and forcing my chin up so he can kiss me, as my cheeks burn red with embarrassment.

"No, I'll call a cab," I argue.

"Go take a shower Priss," he orders, in that tone I just don't seem to be able to disobey. "Then we can eat before Fitzy helps you with some clothes."

As soon as he releases me I dart away, shutting and locking the bathroom door the moment I'm safely inside. My heart is racing, my head spinning with everything that's happened in the last couple of hours. Carson told me he likes me, or maybe he only likes me when we're having sex.

Honestly, I'm not sure and I'm not sure why I'm okay with that. Maybe it's that I think I like him too. Who am I kidding, I know I like him, if I didn't I wouldn't keep letting him invade my life the way he is.

Without my parents I'm floundering, but Carson grounds me. He tells me what he needs, what he expects and I need those rules, I need that guidance, because when I'm doing as he tells me I feel calm and safe.

My hands are shaking as I turn the shower on. They shake the whole time that I wash, leaving my hair smelling of Carson's shampoo. Carefully I unlock the bathroom door, and wrapped only in a towel, I creep into his bedroom. Just like he said he would, he's left a white button-down shirt out for me to wear, but as I slide it over my head I'm all too aware that I'm still naked beneath it, my handful of underwear in the dresser at the hotel.

The shirt reaches almost to my knees, but I still wish it were longer. Grabbing the hairbrush Carson left out, I brush my hair, dragging the tangles free, and then quickly twist it into a braid that hangs over my shoulder.

Sinking down onto the bed, I seriously consider calling a cab and running, but I know I won't. I don't want to leave. I don't want to leave him, even though I know I should.

His words earlier completely disarmed me and now I'm caught, lost to his web, helpless, but a willing victim.

Nineteen

B oth Fitzy and I stay silent until we hear the shower
turn on.

"What the hell are you playing at?" Fitzy hisses.

"What do you mean?" I ask, playing stupid, like I have no
idea what he's talking about.

"That," he hisses, pointing in the direction of the
bedroom, "is Tally's sister. Her *evil*," he emphasizes the
word, "twin sister."

"I know who she is," I reply, reaching into the refrigerator
and pulling two cold beers out, handing one to a consternated
looking Fitzy.

"Does Tally know? Does Arlo know?"

"No. But it's not what you think. Carrigan is the reason
the will is broken."

"It's not what I think?" he whisper-shrieks. "I think
you're sleeping with the enemy."

"She's not the enemy, at least not anymore. She fixed
everything, Tally's free, the Archibald's are gone."

"And Carrigan did that?" he asks slowly.

"Yes, she did it to save them both. Now their parents have

fucked off overseas and they've banned Carrigan from the house, she literally has nothing. No clothes, none of her things, nothing. Tally and Arlo asked her to move in with them, but she's prickly. More than prickly, honestly she's a bitch, but…" I trail off, unsure how to explain her, and this thing between us.

"Hmm," Fitzy says, his eyes narrowing as he assesses me.

"What?" I ask.

"Nothing," he says with an unnerving smile. "Did you mention you were cooking? I'm starved. And for goodness sake Carson go and put some clothes on."

Laughing I excuse myself for a second, and walk into the bedroom, glancing at the closed bathroom door as I pull on some sweatpants and lay out one of my button downs out on the bed for Priss. I'm a little too eager to see her in my clothes again, or maybe it's knowing she'll *only* be wearing my shirt that's got me riled up.

Retreating back to the kitchen I find Fitzy hauling a rail of clothes across the deck. "How the hell did you get that up the gangplank?" I yell, pulling more things from the refrigerator and adding them to the pile I started earlier, before I had Priss shaped desert. I start to chop the veggies, pulling a wok out and quickly throwing together a stir-fry.

"I'm a stylist, that doesn't make me incapable," he says, rolling his eyes dramatically.

Stirring the veggies, I add some chicken to the pan and then a satay sauce, inhaling deeply when the rich peanut scent fills the air. I freeze when the shower turns off, glancing toward the bedroom, then back to a smirking Fitzy who has taken a seat at the island across from me.

"Oh this is fun," he says, winking playfully.

"Shut up," I scold, refocusing my attention on the food cooking in the pan. If Fitzy wasn't here I'd be in there with her, licking the droplets of water from her naked body before I got her all dirty again.

When the food is ready, I split it between three plates, grabbing silverware for all of us and a bottle of water for Priss. I wait a minute longer, expecting her to appear, but the door remains shut and for a moment I panic that she's run again. "I'll go fetch her," I say, scowling at a still smirking Fitzy.

Crossing the galley to my bedroom, I consider knocking, but if she's naked I don't want to give her chance to cover up her beautiful body. Pushing the door open I step into the room and find her sitting on the end of the bed wearing my shirt. She's twisted her hair into a simple braid that's fallen over her shoulder and made the cotton of my shirt almost transparent beneath it. She looks young and scared.

"You okay?" I ask.

She nods, but it's not exactly convincing.

"What's up?"

"I'm trying to convince myself to run," she says, shocking the hell out of me with her honesty.

"I figured as much," I say, sitting down next to her.

"What are we doing?" she asks, her eyes begging me to explain, but the problem is I'm as clueless as she is.

"No fucking clue, but I don't plan to stop."

"Tell me what to do Carson," she begs, tears filling her eyes. "I need someone to tell me what to do, because I don't know how to be anything other than what they told me to be."

Our eyes lock and for the very first time I feel like I understand the girl next to me. So I nod, lift my hand, and pinch her chin between my thumb and forefinger. "Come eat dinner, then let Fitzy help you."

Docilly she nods, mouthing "Thank you," to me, before she pushes to her feet and follows me out the room.

"Goodness me, you are so beautiful and so tiny," Fitzy gushes, as Priss pads barefoot into the kitchen.

Her fingers move to her braid and she fidgets uncomfortably. "I look better with my hair and makeup done," she says.

"Nonsense, you're gorgeous just as you are. Sit, eat, then tell me a little about your style," Fitzy says, doing his best to put her at ease, talking quietly like you would to a skittish animal.

"I wear a lot of dresses," Priss says, carefully tucking my shirt beneath her as she climbs up onto the stool opposite Fitzy's.

"Is that because you like them, or because your mom liked them?" I question, not looking at her as I place her plate full of stir fry in front of her.

"I…" she says, her cheeks coloring pink.

"With those legs you can wear anything you want," Fitzy says quickly, flashing me a glare before he focusses back on Priss.

Sitting down next to her, I lay my palm on her leg, rubbing my thumb back and forth over the skin on her thigh. She tenses for a moment, then relaxes beneath my touch and I lift my fork and eat with my free hand.

Fitzy begins to eat and I watch from the corner of my eye as Priss tentatively lifts her fork.

"What's in here?" she asks.

"Dinner, it's chicken satay stir-fry," I say stabbing a piece of chicken and bringing it to my lips.

"I—" she starts.

"Eat it Priss," I say, an order, not a suggestion.

She faulters, but only for a second before she slowly spears a baby corn and brings it to her lips, biting carefully.

When she takes a second bite, I stop watching and start eating again.

"So, dresses," Fitzy says, clearing his throat, his gaze bouncing between me and the girl beside me.

"My mom liked me to wear dresses most of the time," Priss confesses.

"And do you like dresses?" he asks kindly, his attention on his food.

"I," she pauses, thinking. "I- I don't know."

Fitzy's expression softens. "Well I can help with that."

For the next several minutes we eat while Fitzy tries to get her to chat, but after a second my Priss disappears and Carrigan emerges. Her answers become practiced and polite, robotic, orchestrated and I fucking hate it.

My hand slides from her leg and I lean away from her, unwilling to pretend, wanting *my girl* back. Her eyes snap to me, and I can see the confusion in them. She doesn't know she's gone from sweet and sincere to Carriganbot and for the first time I truly see how ingrained her indoctrination is. It's more than just manners and behaviors, this is a whole separate personality that she switches on and off and I don't think she's even aware.

I may not like the cold, impersonal side of her, but right now she isn't being cruel or bitchy, she isn't trying to manipulate Fitzy, she's just behaving in the way she's be taught to behave. The realization is startling and so obvious that I feel stupid for not seeing it earlier.

Tally has been telling us all along that her twin is as much a victim as she was of their parents' malice and we all denied it, but she was right. Where Tally was ignored, Carrigan was bombarded, where Tally was forced to pretend to be Carrigan, her sister was forced into a mold of their parents' creation.

Both girls have been abused by their parents, just in completely different ways.

Carrigan isn't innocent, just like she told us, she's played the game, did as she was told, but just like Tally, Carrigan is much more resilient than you'd expect. The sweet girl, the one I like, the one I crave, is still there beneath the façade of polished creation, despite the girl's parents' best efforts to make her just as heartless and evil as they are.

Leaning down I press a kiss to her shoulder, and like my touch flipped a switch she faulters, some of the polish falling from her voice as Priss reappears. Her softened gaze looks to me and a small, sad smile hitches the side of her beautiful lips.

Carrigan Archibald is a complicated, fucked up, beautiful mess and I want her, all of her. I'm rarely a selfish person, but I'm rich enough, stubborn enough, and controlling enough to know that she's my new obsession and whether she knows it or not, she's mine.

Twenty

CARRIGAN

EST 1917

W hen I'm around Carson I swear food tastes better. The plate full of rich nutty chicken, noodles, and veggies is delicious and before I'm even aware that I've done it, I've eaten every bite. I understand hunger far too well, but I'm not familiar with this warm feeling of fullness I get whenever I eat with Carson. It might just be that the food he eats is so bad for me that I'm bloated and full of carbs and sugar, but for the first time I'm starting to understand the enjoyment in good food.

Until him, I thought boys were simple. My mom explained how to play with them, how to tease, to coax, to lead them around with promises that I was never going to fulfil. But Carson isn't like any of the rest of them. He doesn't react the way he should.

When I'm the Carrigan I was taught to be, he's cold and disinterested, but then when I feel at my weakest, in the moments that I'm too sad and pathetic and feeble to be the person I'm expected to be, he's sweet and affectionate.

I don't understand.

"When you're acting like you think Carrigan Archibald

ought to act, I call you Carrigan. When you're acting like the girl who gave me her virginity, the one I want to be around, the one I can't keep away from, I call you Priss."

Those were his words, like I have a split personality or something, like I can control it.

Fitzy's been asking me questions all through dinner, but I don't know what answers they expect me to give. I don't know who I am, I don't know what I like, all I am is who I was told to be, but I can't admit that.

"Right," Fitzy announces, pushing off his stool with a bright smile. "I didn't know your exact measurements, so some of the things I bought won't fit, but how about we try some things on, so you can see if you like them?" he suggests.

"Okay, thank you."

"I have a few more bits that I think might work in the car, I'll just go grab them and the changing screen," he says, as he disappears back outside.

When it's just Carson and me, I feel the weight of his eyes on me and this pressure to be who he wants me to be settles on my shoulders. Sometimes being near him is easy, but other times like now it's hard. I don't know what he expects of me. He likes to be in charge and like earlier when I was feeling weak, I needed him to take control. But he's not my friend or boyfriend or fiancé, he's just someone I have sex with and I need to remember that.

Sliding off my stood, I look around the small kitchen space. At home we had staff to collect plates and do whatever they do with them, but I haven't seen anyone here other than him on either occasion I've been here. "Thank you for dinner," I say politely. "Do you have a dishwasher, or something?" I ask, feeling foolish.

"Have you ever used a dishwasher?" he asks, his lips quirking up into a smile.

"No, but—"

"Come here baby," he says, beckoning me toward him.

Sighing I stay put, wrapping one arm around my waist. "Look Carson."

"No," he says decisively, cutting me off before I have a chance to speak. "I like you Priss."

"All of me, or just the Priss parts?" I ask, shocking myself.

Reaching out, he snags my wrist, encircling it with his fingers and then slowly reeling me toward him. "I like you when you're disarmed, when you're not playing games, when you're real. I like your body, I like the way you melt beneath me, and next to me, whenever I have my hands on you. I like how soft you are when you let that hard, practiced shell dissolve. I like that you let me take charge and that you like it too. I don't want or need anything from you, I just fucking like you Carrigan," he says, oh so softly, his lips a hairs breath away from mine.

"I—"

His lips press against mine before I can speak again and he kisses me, slowly moving his mouth against mine in a way that's different to the others we've shared. This kiss isn't about lust or want, it feels more indulgent, like he's kissing me just because he likes me and he wants to and I don't ever want it to stop.

The noise of a throat being cleared shatters the moment and I go to lurch away from him, but he doesn't let me, kissing me for a moment longer before he slowly pulls his lips from mine, still holding me close as he turns his attention to Fitzy.

"You ready to pick some clothes?" Fitzy says, with a smirk.

"Sure," I say, with a nod, reluctantly stepping away from Carson.

Fitzy sets up a large screen in the corner of the living room area and motions for me to step behind it. "Okay, Carson told me your size, and I'm a pretty good judge, so I think these should fit," he says, handing me a bra and panties set made of pale blue satin, edged with soft lace.

It's not a color I'd normally wear, but once it's on I love the way it looks against my skin and I'm amazed to find it fits perfectly.

"Right, since we spoke about dresses I thought we could start there," Fitzy says from the other side of the screen a moment before a garment bag appears.

Unzipping it I pull out a deep emerald green dress and slip it over my head. Fitted around my torso, it has capped sleeves and flares slightly from the waist with a triangular cut out section that reveals a small glimpse of the skin between my breasts and stomach. It's exactly something my mom would choose.

"How does it fit?" he asks.

"It's fits perfectly," I say and it does.

"Can I see?" he asks.

Stepping out from behind the screen I find Fitzy waiting a few paces away and Carson sat on the couch, a beer in hand, his eyes on me.

"What do you think?" Fitzy asks, pulling my attention back to him.

"It's nice," I say noncommittally.

"Nice," Fitzy says, rolling the word across his tongue. "So it's a no?"

"No. I don't know. What do you think?" I ask him.

His eyes go sad and he crosses toward me, wrapping me in an unexpected hug. His build is much leaner than Carson's but still solid and firm. When he pulls back he doesn't release me completely, his fingers running along the end of my braid. "Oh sweet girl," he coos.

"I'm not sweet," I tell him quietly. "That's my sister."

"No honey, that's you too. You're even more broken than she is, aren't you?"

"I'm not broken, I'm just evil," I breath.

He shakes his head. "Oh Carrigan, the bruises are just below the surface for you aren't they," he whispers quietly.

A tear escapes from my eye and rolls down my cheek as I stare at this man who I just met, but who sees me in a way that I don't see myself, he sees something in me that's not bad and twisted.

I hear Carson moving behind us and so must Fitzy, because he clears his throat and smiles. "That dress is a no. Unless it wows you and makes you feel beautiful, it's not for you."

Letting him guide me back behind the screen, I wipe the tears from my cheeks as I strip the dress off and try on the next outfit he hands me. An hour later I've discovered that I like skirts, the color blue, and blazers, and I have a real smile on my face for the first time in longer than I can remember.

Back home I have closets full of clothes, and I've always endured shopping rather than enjoyed it. But trying on all these outfits with Fitzy has been fun. His enthusiasm for clothes is overwhelming and with his sweet guiding help I think I'm starting to figure out what I like.

I expected Carson to leave, he's a guy after all, what guy enjoys clothes. But the entire time I've been trying on outfits, he's stayed in the living room, his feet propped up on the coffee table watching me, smiling as I smile, not giving an opinion until I'd given my own.

"Thank you," I say to Fitzy, as he collapses the privacy screen.

"Pah, this is what I live for," he says, waving my thanks off. "I'll be back the day after tomorrow with some more choices for you now we're getting a firmer fix on your style and I have your proper measurements, then going forward I'll just send things out to you as I find them for you."

"I'm not sure where I'm going to be staying, but for the moment I'm at the Haywood Hotel. Do you bill me, or should I give you my credit card details? How does this work?" I ask.

"Oh it's already sorted," Fitzy says, leaning in to press a kiss against my cheek. "And I have your cell number so I'll just text you and you can let me know where you want me to bring the next batch of things for you to try."

"How is it sorted? Are you going to send the bill to the hotel?" I ask, narrowing my eyes a little. The outfits we picked together tonight are thousands of dollars' worth of clothes, I mean I know he knows I'm rich, but I still need to know how to pay him.

"He's putting it on my account," Carson says.

"What, why?" I gasp, spinning to face him.

"Because I told him to."

"Right my darlings," Fitzy interrupts, "I'll leave you to it. Carrigan, it was a pleasure to meet you, I'll see you soon."

"Thank you, man," Carson says, embracing Fitzy in a man hug, before the older man leaves pulling the rail of clothes behind him.

I wait for a moment, until Fitzy is out of sight before I turn on Carson. "What are you doing?"

"Come here Priss."

"No," I snap, crossing my arms across my chest and holding my ground. "You can't just buy my clothes."

"Why not?" he asks calmly, closing the distance between us, ignoring my obvious annoyance.

"Because you can't, people don't just buy other people a whole new wardrobe," I say, uncrossing then re-crossing my arms, fidgeting beneath his unwavering gaze.

"I really couldn't give a fuck what other people do. I wanted to do this, so I did," he says, his expression intense, but calm.

"I have money," I insist.

"I know, we all have money, more than we'll ever need."

"So I don't need you to pay for my things."

"I know that. But I'm still going to," he says, reaching for me and pulling me to him. "The customary response to a gift is thank you."

"Carson."

His sigh is loud. "Priss, just say thank you, then kiss me."

Wary, I stare at him for a long moment, trying to understand his motives, what he thinks this gift is going to get him, what game this is.

"Jesus," he mutters, a second before he palms the back of my head and pulls my lips up to his.

Mom always taught me that every interaction with a boy had purpose, that I should use it to my advantage. A shy look here, a soft touch there. She promised me I could make them all fall in love with me, if I just learnt their weak spots. I know how to play with a guy, but always on my terms and it's never more than a means of getting what I want.

Only all those things don't apply to Carson, do they? The money is gone, he knows that, he helped me get out from beneath its burden, so what game is he playing?

Am I playing with him?

No.

How can I be manipulating him, when I literally have no idea what's going on?

"Stop thinking," Carson growls against my lips a second before he reclaims them, teasing me into losing myself to his touch like he does every time he's near me.

Allowing myself to just give in, I enjoy him, enjoy the way his huge body makes me feel small and protected. I enjoy how he holds me tight against him, like he doesn't want me to escape, and how when I'm in his arms I feel like it's possible to just be me. Be who I am in this moment and not a product of my past, and that maybe, just maybe, I can forge a better future for myself.

When he pulls back, I reluctantly release my hold on him, not realizing that my fingers were clinging to him. "Thank you," I whisper.

I feel his smile against my forehead when he presses a soft, barely there, kiss against me. "You're welcome Priss."

"I should go," I tell him, not wanting to leave, but not wanting to overstay my welcome either.

"Or you could stay," he says, pulling away until I'm looking up into his handsome face.

"I don't understand? We already had sex," I say, bewildered. Does he want to do it again? I mean I'm okay with that, but is that what he means.

"I love fucking you Priss, but that isn't the only reason I want you to stay with me," he says, his fingers gripping my chin, holding my face up when all I want to do is look away.

"Then why?"

A sadness fills his eyes and I instantly prickle, I don't want his pity.

"Have you ever had a boyfriend?"

I shake my head.

"Ever had a guy friend?"

I shake my head again.

"Ever had a friend."

Scowling, I rip my chin from his grip and try to turn away, but he grabs me, hauling me roughly back to him. He forces me to walk backwards, crowding me until my spine hits the wall and he cages me in, his body pressed firm against mine, imprisoning me.

"Don't fucking turn away from me when I'm talking to you. When we're having a conversation I want to see your eyes. You get me?" he snarls, eyes angry and daring me to look away.

I nod. "Okay," I whisper. What he's doing, how he's acting, I should be frightened, but he's not hurting me. If I really wanted to leave I think he'd let me despite our size difference, because even though he's huge and has me pinned to a wall, I feel utterly protected by him.

"Good. Now listen to me carefully, because I'm going to spell it out for you. *I like you.* I want to figure you out. Yes, I want to fuck you. Yes, I want to kiss and touch you and watch you do what I ask you to, but that's not all I want."

I feel my lips part in shock, but no sound comes out as I watch him swallow, his head tilting to the side a little as he stares at me.

"I don't understand it Priss, but I want to take care of you. I want to protect you and look after you. I think I want to fucking keep you, which is confusing the fucking hell out of me, but the truth is that I don't think you're evil. I don't think you're a bad person."

I open my mouth to speak but he glares, shaking his head to silence me.

"I'm not an idiot. I know you've done bad shit. I know you've used and manipulated and lied. I know you've done stuff that has tarnished you. But the things you've done don't have to define you, not if you learn from them."

His words are honest and brutal, but his touch is so soft I barely realized that he's stroking my cheek until he's stopped speaking and is just watching me.

"I'll take you back to the hotel, but I want you to think about what I've said. You don't have to be alone Priss. Your sister wants a relationship with you, she wants to be in your life. I want to be in your life. Hell, after one night I can guarantee that Fitzy wants to be in your life, and all you have to do is let us. I won't tell you what to do about this Priss, even though I can see from the way you're looking at me that you want me to. This has to be your decision."

"I'm not a good person to be around, I don't trust who I am," I admit, closing my eyes so I don't have to see his face.

"So choose to be different. Choose to be a sister, choose to be a friend, choose to be mine. But whatever you do, *you* have to be the one to choose it. You. Not your mom and dad, not some dead guy, not me. You."

I have no idea what's happening tonight. Honestly, I have no idea what's been happening since I woke up to find her in my bedroom asking me to help her break that godforsaken will.

Everything that's happened since that day has been like a river full of rapids, never stopping, just bouncing me from one eddy to the next while I frantically try to keep my head above water.

Carrigan Archibald is the enemy.

Was the enemy.

Now, I have no fucking clue what she is.

No that's a lie, I know what I want her to be. I want her to be mine, my Priss, mine. But what the hell would I do with her if she was? Can I even tell my friends, my family that I fell for the devil? Only she's not the devil, she's just a lonely, mixed up sad girl. When I met Tally, I thought she was the saddest person I'd ever met, but behind the fragile exterior is a backbone of steel. Her twin is the opposite, her exterior is hard, but her inside is soft and delicate. Two sides of the same coin and somehow, I've lost myself to them both. Tally as a sister, Priss as my girl.

My girl.

I want Carrigan Archibald to be my girl. Only instead of carrying her to my bed, I'm walking her to her hotel room and I'm going to have to leave her here, even though I hate it, even though I want her to sleep naked and curled against me.

I can't make her choose to live, to change, to take responsibility for her past and then move forward from it. If I could take that burden for her I would, but I can't, so instead I'm going to walk away and hope she finds her way back to me, even though it's going to kill me to do it.

She hasn't said a word since I pinned her to the fucking wall of my boat like a god damn caveman. She just silently gathered her cell and the robe she was wearing when I hauled her from her bedroom and then followed me to the car. She's wearing one of the outfits Fitzy bought over, a soft pink blouse and tight white jeans, that make her look tiny and curvy all at the same time.

Wedged sandals raise her up so she can almost look me in the eye without tipping her head back. Her hair is still in a braid and her face still bare of makeup. She looks fucking gorgeous, but as much as I want to, I won't touch her.

Taking her key card from her hand I open the door and hover in the corridor while she walks past me and into the small room. "Night Priss," I say quietly, tensing my muscles to stop myself from reaching for her.

"Goodnight Carson," she whispers, her hand curling around the door handle.

"I'll leave you alone, okay? Think about what I said and then come find me," I tell her, forcing myself to turn and walk away, even though it's literally the last thing I want, knowing that she might never talk to me again.

I can't do to her what her parents did, I can't take advantage of her naturally compliant nature. If she comes to me, if she goes to Tally, it has to be her decision, her choice.

F our days. That's how long I sit in my hotel room, trying to figure out what to do; who I am and who I want to be.

Four days without seeing or hearing from Carson.

Four days without feeling whole.

Four days is how long it takes me to stop moping and become irrationally angry. Angry at him for making me think, angry at myself for being so weak that I hadn't figured this out for myself. But mainly I'm angry at my parents. I'm angry that they were as complicit in everything I did as I was, but that they get to run away and leave me to deal with the consequences alone. I'm angry that they didn't take me with them and I'm angry that I want to go.

Four days is how long this anger and fury festers inside of me before I start to do something.

Snatching up the hotel telephone I dial down to reception.

"Haywood Hotel, how may I assist you?" the cheerful voice asks.

"Can I have the biggest ice cream sundae you do and a martini, extra dry please?" I ask, smiling manically as I order things that I would never have been allowed if my mom was here.

"Of course, I'll have room service bring that up to your room, is there anything else I can help you with?"

"No thank you."

"Okay, thank you ma'am."

Placing the receiver down, I jump up from the bed, suddenly too agitated to sit still for a moment longer. Glancing down at the robe I'm wearing, I frown. How long was I really planning on hiding in this room, basking in my misery? Ripping the robe off, I throw it to the floor and head for the bathroom, letting the hot shower wash all of my pathetic mopiness down the drain. When I emerge, pink skinned, I pull on the outfit I wore home from Carson's the other night, turning to assess myself in the mirror.

The blouse is my signature pink color, but my mom would hate this outfit, which only makes me love it more. Twisting to the side I take in my reflection, I look like me, only different. My eyes are bright but full of sadness and regret. I don't want to be this person, this pathetic, weak creature that hides from life.

The time for feeling sorry for myself has passed, my sister forced herself out from the shadows and bloomed in the sunlight, and now she's happy and in love and free, and I want that too. I broke that will, but I'm still shackled to it by regret, guilt, and loss. I need to move on. Carson was right, he told me I could choose who to be, only he couldn't make this decision for me, I needed to find my way here on my own.

A knock at the door heralds the arrival of my food and I throw it open and invite the server in, adding a large tip to the bill before closing the door behind him and diving for my ice cream. The cold vanilla coats my mouth, making each taste bud burst to life as I groan around the spoon. Each mouthful tastes like rebellion and happiness and life. It's the most delicious thing I've ever tasted, and by the time I'm scaping the last bite from the bottom of the glass I know what I need to do.

It's time to reclaim my life, forge a new future for myself and stop living in the past. My parents were wrong, I have value and worth beyond that inheritance. If Tally can find happiness, maybe I can find a way to atone for my sins and perhaps seek a little revenge on the way.

The car service pulls into the St Augustus drive and I pull in a reaffirming breath. Today, for the first time, I want to be here, but that doesn't make walking the halls of the school any less nerve wracking.

Squeezing my fingers together into fists I try to stop the trembling in my hands. For years St Augustus has been my domain. When I walk down the halls people stop and stare, it used to be because I was on the verge of inheriting a fortune, but today I plan to make them stop and turn for a different reason.

Instead of trying to sneak in without anyone noticing, I've timed my entrance so everyone will see me. Today I won't hide from their penetrating stares, it's time to reclaim my identity and this is the first step. When the car pulls to a stop a few feet from the entrance steps I pull in a deep breath, lift my chin, and remind myself who I am.

I'm Carrigan Prudence Archibald and I gave up billions of dollars to save myself and my twin sister. I'm not perfect and I've done truly awful things, but I won't cower away from my actions.

The door opens and I only pause for a second before I

twist in my seat, dropping my feet to the floor, then I rise to my full height. Lifting my eyes, I smirk at the onlookers whose mouths fall open.

Gone is my poker straight, honey blonde hair, replaced with platinum blonde, textured waves that frame my face in a sexily disheveled way. Gone is the natural, flawless makeup my mom painstakingly taught me how to perfect, replaced with a nude lip and dark eye liner that makes my blue eyes seem twice as big. Gone is the conservative knee length skirt chosen to remind everyone that my virtue is intact, replaced with the mid-thigh version that Carson flipped up while he fucked me over a couch just a few days ago.

Each of my steps is purposeful and full of renewed confidence. I'm still me, only this version I like, this version I chose. This isn't my parents' image of me, this is who I'm deciding to be and it feels like with each step I take I shed more of the weight of shame and expectation that's been holding me hostage.

Today I'm telling the all too familiar eyes on me that I won't cower, that I'm no longer ashamed. For the first time since I gave up a fortune I feel like me again, and my classmates and everyone else who watches me go knows it too. The other students and their opinions aren't important anymore. There's only a handful of people at St Augustus that I want to see and it's time to find them.

"Carrigan," my sister says, her mouth falling open for a second before it curves into a wide smile. "I love the new look."

"Thanks," I say, lifting my hand to flip the hair that's fallen into my eyes out of the way.

"Are you okay?" she asks, cautiously.

"Yeah, I am, I think. Could we talk?"

"Of course," she says, her grin widening.

"Later, somewhere private, the others too."

"Do you want to come to Arlo's place?"

"No, how about Carson's boat?" I suggest.

"What about my boat?" Carson asks from behind me.

My body tingles with excitement just from the sound of his voice, but I don't turn to face him, not yet.

"Carrigan wants to talk to us all, she wondered if we could use your boat," Tally says sweetly, a tinge of suspicious filling her voice.

"Is that what you want Carrigan?" Carson says, his voice low and gruff.

Inhaling sharply, I spin around to face him. "If that would be okay?"

His eyes rake over my hair and face, and one side of his mouth lifts up into a half smile. "Of course, you can have whatever you want, all you have to do is ask."

My lips twitch up into a smile and I move without thought, launching myself at him and pressing my lips to his. Wrapping his arms around me, he binds me to him as he takes control of the kiss, devouring my lips, while his fingers tangle with my hair. Gripping me tightly, he holds me in place, showing me and anyone else who's watching that I'm indisputably his.

"What the fuck?" I hear someone say, but we don't even pause, kissing each other like we'll never get another chance. Eventually Carson pulls away, not letting me go, but allowing me a tiny amount of room to breathe.

"Tally, I need to the key," he snaps.

"What?" she asks slowly.

"The dark room, I need the key," he says, not even trying to hide the need in his voice.

I try to turn to look at my sister but Carson claims my lips again stopping me.

"Thank you," he says, barely tearing his mouth from mine long enough to speak, before he's lifting me off the ground and we're moving, his hands on the back of my thighs as he urges my legs around his waist.

Moments later we're moving through the door to the dark room and my back hits the cushions of the couch as he follows me down, kissing me, his hands running over me like he never thought he'd get the chance to do it again.

"Carson," I gasp, as his lips reach my neck, his teeth nipping at my skin.

"Are you mine Priss?" he demands.

"Carson."

"I asked you a fucking question. Are you mine?" he snarls, saying each word slowly, between bites.

Am I his? I don't even have to think about it, I've been his since the first time he called me Priss, from the first moment that he looked at me and saw who I could be. "Yes, yes," I gasp.

Then we're a blur of motion, fingers, lips, kisses, nips all mingled with my moans and cries and his groans of pleasure. He touches me like I'm special, like I'm important, like I'm his, and I worship him like he's mine, like he's the first, the last, and the only one in between and none of it's a game, none of it's a manipulation or a coercion. Everything between us is real and by the time we're naked and panting, entwined together on the couch, nothing has ever felt more real and right and honest to me.

Her white blonde hair is rested against my chest, her tits heaving up and down as she pants, her body damp with sweat, soft and pliant against me.

Mine.

The word settles into my core and calms me. I didn't realize how desperate I was for some claim on her, some sense of ownership, until now. She kissed me, right there in front of her sister and half the fucking school. She kissed me. I think that's the first time she's ever made the first move, to be the one to instigate things.

When I left the hotel the other night, I'd about convinced myself that she'd never speak to me again and the last five days have been hell, as I've convinced myself not to railroad her life and take control. She needed to get here on her own.

"I like the new look," I tell her, resting my chin against the top of her head,

"Thanks," she giggles and I love the way it sounds on her. Happy and young.

"So what you been up to the last few days?" I ask, trying to sound nonchalant and failing miserably.

Pulling away from me, she sits up and turns to face me, not trying to hide her nakedness from me. "Mainly I sulked and moped."

A laugh falls from my lips and I sit up, resting my back against the arm of the couch. "Yeah?"

"Yep. Then yesterday I got really angry."

"At what?" I ask.

"Pretty much everything. Me, my mom and dad. You."

"Me?" I ask, smiling.

"Yeah you." Closing her eyes, she pulls in a slow breath. "I like you Carson and that scares the hell out of me. You make me feel weird and warm and I have no idea what to do with that, and I'm mad at you because I was content to exist in my bubble of shame and you wouldn't let me."

"I'm not gonna apologize," I say, smiling, as I reach out and tuck a strand of her hair behind her ear.

"I don't expect you to. But you need to take off the rose tinted glasses and stop pretending that I'm not a bitch. I am and that's not because my mom told me to be, that's just because I really am a bitch."

"I know you're a bitch Priss," I say, tweaking her nipple between my finger and thumb. "You can be as bitchy as you like, to whoever you want, except me and your sister, she doesn't deserve it and I won't allow it."

"You won't allow it?" she says, arching an eyebrow at me.

"Nope," I say, launching myself forward and pushing her back down against the couch as I crawl over her, caging her in with my arms and pinning her body down with my own, my hard dick grinding against her wet pussy. "I'll fuck the bitchiness out of you."

"That doesn't sound so bad," she purrs.

"It will when I don't let you come, pushing you to the

edge over and over and never letting you fall off," I growl, grinding my hips and letting the tip of my dick push into her.

Her legs lift, wrapping around my back, her heels digging into my ass, urging me deeper, but I don't move, giving her only the shallowest of thrusts, teasing her.

"Carson," she whines, lifting her hips up.

"I think you forgot how this works. I'm in control."

"So be in control, I'm yours," she says, her words so much more impactful than the blasé way she just offered them.

"Say it again," I growl.

Her beautiful blue eyes blink up at me, her lips parting slightly as they curve into a grin. "I'm yours," she whispers.

I slam home, filling her in one hard thrust and claiming her completely, my lips taking hers as I seal her words with a kiss. By the time we peel ourselves free of each other its lunchtime and we've missed all our morning classes. Her hair is messy, her makeup smudged, but she's never looked sexier to me.

"What are we going to tell my sister?" she asks, her arms banded around my waist as we sneak out of the dark room and into the empty hallway.

"That we're together."

"And are we?" she asks, sounding like she genuinely isn't sure.

Spinning her in my arms, I cup her face with my hands and roll my eyes. "Yes Carrigan, we're together. You're mine and I'm yours. Boyfriend and girlfriend, a couple or whatever else you want to call us. Okay?"

"Okay," she says, smiling as I tuck her under my arm and guide her towards the cafeteria.

"We thought you'd skipped," Wats says, his grin wide and salacious.

"No we're still here," I say, leaning forward and slugging him in the shoulder without releasing my hold on Priss.

"Ow," he laughs, rubbing at his shoulder, before turning calculating eyes to the girl at my side. "You lowering yourself to eat with us today Carrigan, now you're sucking Carson's dick?"

A coldness radiates through me as my muscles tense and I ready myself to beat the living shit out of my friend.

"Watson," she purrs, untangling herself from my arm and taking a step toward him.

"What's up boo, you hoping to take a ride on us all?" he sneers.

Her heels click along the floor as she closes the distance between them. I feel myself tense as she places her bright pink nails against his chest, tilts her head to the side and whispers just loud enough for me to hear. "Go fuck yourself." A second before she snaps her knee up and into his balls.

A startled laugh falls from my lips as Watson crumples to a heap at her feet. "Dude," I hiss, laughing as my balls clench up in sympathy. Priss walks straight back into my arms and I feel myself relax. I might be falling for her, but she's still an enigma and a serious flight risk.

Wats curls into a ball on the floor, his hands covering his balls as he groans.

"What did Wats do?" Tally asks, arriving at our side, Arlo's arm curled around her neck possessively.

"He deserved it," Priss says quickly, her teeth worrying at her lower lip.

"I've no doubt," Tally says shrugging it off with a laugh.

"What the fuck is going on with you guys?" Arlo asks, his expression suspicious as he looks between me and Priss, who is clinging to me, some of her earlier confidence fading.

"Let's skip and we can go back to The Escape," I suggest,

looking down to Priss, who nods her agreement. Unable to resist I lift her chin and press my lips against hers.

Priss rides with me, while the others follow in Arlo's car, he started driving himself once he and Tally made it official. I can feel the tension radiating off Priss as we drive the familiar route to the marina, but she's stoically silent at my side. "You okay?" I ask.

"Kind of," she answers, not elaborating.

"That a good or bad *kind of*?"

"I had this big plan to march into school and talk to my sister and then you were there and I kissed you and then we, you know, and you stole all my sass and now I don't think I can do what I planned to do," she garbles, talking so quickly I can barely keep up.

"I gotta be honest, I'm not sorry about the kissing and fucking."

She laughs lightly, shaking her head as she stares out the windscreen.

"What did you plan to do?" I ask, wanting to keep her talking.

"Something that seemed like a good idea last night when I was full of bravado, getting my hair bleached, drinking martini's, and eating ice-cream, but it all feels a bit stupid now."

"Tell me, I'm sure it's not stupid," I coax, sliding my hand onto her leg and squeezing.

"I was going to apologize and then I was going to ask for help," she says quietly.

"Baby, that doesn't sound stupid at all."

"It will when I tell you what I wanted help with."

My chest tightens and worry builds inside of me, what the hell could she need help with. If it's leaving, she can forget it, I'm not letting her go anywhere. Fuck I hope it's not with classes, Tally would probably say yes but Arlo would lose his mind. We'll be at the marina in a matter of minutes but I can't wait that long. "What did you need help with?"

For the first time since we got in the car she turns and looks at me, her face so beautiful, the new hair and makeup, combined with the post sex rumpled look only making her more stunning. "Revenge."

I can tell I've shocked him. I've shocked myself that I actually said it, that I'm verbalizing all the garbled angry thoughts that have been swirling around inside of me for the last two days.

His attention turns back to the road for a moment, before he looks at me again, his lips parted as if he's going to speak. The entrance to the marina forces his attention back to the road as he pulls onto to the lot and parks in his usual space.

Arlo's huge SUV pulls up at our side and our moment to talk privately is lost in a flurry of doors opening and us moving as a group toward his boat. Without thought, I enter the galley and move to the huge armchair, kicking off my shoes and curling into the chair as if the huge overstuffed thing can protect me from this stupid meeting that I called.

My plan this morning was to be a total badass, demand a meeting, then run off to have a meltdown that I demanded a meeting. Only of course that didn't happen and instead Carson was there and all my badass melted into a puddle of want and lust and need for him. Now I'm here in the meeting

I asked for, feeling like a fool and wishing I could leave but knowing that I can't, especially not now I jumped into Carson's arms and basically told the whole world I was sleeping with him.

After a few minutes I realize that the room is silent and when I look up, all eyes are on me. I catch Carson's eye and he must see that I'm struggling because he marches across the room, picks me up out the chair and sits back down with me in his lap.

"Carrigan and I fucked to break the will," he announces, as calmly as if he just asked what the time was.

"Carson," I gasp, shocked that he just announced it, just like that.

Olly's hyena laugh is loud and so compelling that even though I'm horrified, I can't help but want to smile until Tally reaches over and slaps him to make him shut up.

Turning, I glare at Carson, but he just shrugs at me completely unapologetic.

"I like her, she likes me, we're together. Anyone got a problem with that?" he asks boldly, looking between his friends and waiting for them to say something.

Glancing at my sister I find her face buried in her hands, but I can still see the pink embarrassed tinge to her skin. I don't know if she's embarrassed that we fucked, or that he just blurted it out, but either way I open my mouth to speak.

"But she's a bitch, she's the enemy," Watsons says.

The need to defend myself surges forward and I move to stand, but Carson's arm bands around my waist stopping me.

"The only people she did any wrong to in this room are Tally and Arlo. But she put that right, she broke the will, fucking herself over in the process," Carson argues.

"Look," I say interrupting him. "I am a bitch, I don't deny

that. I've definitely done unforgivable, evil things, but I'm trying to change. What happened to Tallulah made me really see what we were doing."

"Stop," my sister shouts. "Carrigan you don't have to explain yourself to him. You saved me, you saved both of us and as far as I'm concerned we're good, you're my twin," she implores.

Ignoring everyone else, I focus on my sister. "I'm so sorry. I don't think I've actually told you how sorry I am. I was so jealous of you our entire lives and then the will happened and they were interested in me, I was important," I tell her, tears filling my eyes. "I really wanted to be important to them. I'm not trying to excuse everything I've done, but I went from being invisible, to being special. To Mom and Dad lavishing all this attention on me and the more compliant I was, the more I did as they said, the more attentive they were. I knew it was wrong but it wasn't till that day, when they attacked you, that I really saw how toxic our relationship with them was."

"It's okay," Tallulah says.

"No it's not."

"It is, because I think I would have done the same if I'd been the one named in that will," she says quietly, getting up from her chair and moving toward me.

Compelled, I stand too, meeting her half way across the room. "No, you wouldn't," I say as I accept the hug she offers me, carefully wrapping my arms around my twin and taking the comfort she's giving me, even though I don't deserve it.

"Carrigan is going to move in here with me," Carson announces, his posture relaxed as he lounges in the chair I just vacated.

"She's what?" Arlo shouts.

"I'm what?" I cry.

"You're moving in here with me," Carson says, his eyes daring me to argue.

"No, I'm not."

"She can come and stay with us," Arlo says, smiling softly at my sister who is now in his arms.

"She's not moving in with me," Watson says, beneath his breath but loud enough that we can all hear him.

"Fuck you," I snarl in his direction.

"She's moving in here," Carson says again, his tone brooking no argument. "Priss, don't fucking argue, you hate being at the hotel, I hate you being at the hotel, we're together so you're moving in here with me.

My lips part and an argument fills my tongue, but no words come out as I scan the faces of the people in the room, ending with my sister. Tally's eyes narrow a little and she looks from me to Carson and back again, before her lips tip up into a sly smile. "I think you moving onto The Escape with Carson is a great idea."

"You do?" I cry.

"It's perfect," Tally says, flashing a conspiratorial grin at Carson, before turning her attention back to me. "Is that what you wanted to talk to us all about? You and Carson?"

"No," I blurt, suddenly remembering why I planned this meeting to start off with, and how ridiculous it all sounds in the cold, rational light of day.

"So what did you want to talk to us about?" she asks.

"I wanted to talk to you about Mom and Dad," I say quietly, feeling the tension build in the room just from the mention of our parents.

"What the fuck about them?" Arlo growls, pulling my sister into him protectively as if he can shelter her with his arms from whatever it is I plan on saying.

"God this all made so much more sense last night. It seems a bit ridiculous now," I mutter, running my fingers through my hair, absentmindedly trying to make it smooth and perfect.

"Have they been in touch with you?" Tally asks.

"No. God no and I doubt they will," I say quickly. "But last night I got thinking and really none of this seems fair."

"Life isn't fair. Please tell me we aren't here so you could feel sorry for yourself," Watson sneers, his lips twisted into an ugly line as he stares me down.

"Give it a rest Wats. She's Tally's sister, and Carson's girl," Olly says, his tone an unexpected warning.

"I get it Watson you think I deserve it and I'll be the first to admit that everything I'm dealing with now is probably karma's way of getting its own back on me for all the shitty things I've done the last few years. But I'm here trying to make amends, to put my life back together, now that my entire future has been changed," I say.

"You saw how wrong things were and you started to put them right, constantly blaming yourself isn't going to help anything," Tally says, reminding us all why she's the nice twin and I'm not.

"But that's the thing," I announce. "I was thinking that while we're here trying to put our lives back together, they've got off scot free."

"Who? Your parents?" Carson asks.

"Yes. We were kids when all this started. I'm not trying to say it was all them, but they coached me, they drilled those rules into me over and over so they were so ingrained I'll never be able to forget them. Mom told me what to do, what to say, how to behave, she conditioned me to believe that all of our lives would be ruined if we didn't play our part in securing all our futures," I tell them, looking between the faces of the guys in the room, before moving back to my sister.

"They did it to me too," Tally says, her voice quiet and meek. "They made me believe that if I stopped doing what they said, that we'd lose the money and it would all be my fault."

"Exactly, and if we stepped out of line, they doled out the consequences."

"They hit you too?" Carson growls, his voice hard and lethal.

"No," I say, shaking my head.

"They did other stuff, didn't they?" Tally asks, her voice barely above a whisper.

"It doesn't matter," I say, wrapping my arm around myself.

"They starved you," she utters. "And humiliated you and ignored you. I remember," Tally breathes, her voice cracking as she covers her mouth with her hand. "Oh my god they did all of that and I never did anything, they did that for years."

"I want revenge," I shout, needing to silence her, to make her shut up about the things I don't ever want to think about again. "It's not fair that they just get to walk away from this. It's not fair that they get to just pretend we don't exist, that they weren't as complicit in this as I was."

"Carrigan," Tally says moving toward me on wobbly legs.

"No," I shriek, lifting up a hand to ward her away, to stop her from bringing all those memories down on me. "I want them to feel at least a little of what we felt. I want them to understand that they don't get to just forget about us. I want revenge," I cry through a broken sob.

"But they're not here," Olly says quietly.

"I know, and they're still playing with us from the other

side of the world. Because of them we can't go into the house we grew up in, the house we've spent more time in than either of them. Because of them we've had to start over with almost nothing. Because of them we don't have parents, we don't have a family, and it's not fair."

"It's not fair," my twin agrees, nodding her head, even as tears stream down her face.

"I want them to suffer, even if it's only a bit, even if it is only a blip to them. It's not fair that they just get to forget us and everything we've done. I want revenge and you should want it too," I say, imploring her to understand, to feel the way I do.

She nods, slow to start, then getting stronger as she reaches out and takes my hand. "What do you want to do?"

"I have no idea," I say, the sound half laugh, half sob. "But I can't just let them walk away without knowing that I've done something."

"We can do it," Arlo says, moving to Tally's side, becoming yet again her strength and support.

"Hell yeah we can, we're the future generations of the five most powerful old money families, between us we can make them feel this," Olly says, jumping up and coming to join us.

"Oh yes, this is going to be fun," Wats says, laughing manically.

"Let's make them suffer," Carson growls, his palm curling around my nape possessively.

"I want to piss them off, annoy the hell out of them and make them hurt in every way possible. I want them to suffer, I want revenge," I cry, letting my body melt into Carson's strength, knowing without question that he will hold me up, that he will be there.

"Together we can do this. Together we can make them regret being the shittiest parents ever," Tally says, her fingers still entwined with mine, gripping me tightly.

My eyes run over the people in the room, ending on Carson, this boy who should hate me, but doesn't. This boy who helped me, guided me, bossed me around. This boy who I need, who I want, who I like.

"I should have known that day you asked me to help you that I'd lose myself completely to you," he says, his thumb rubbing along my jaw.

"I need your help again," I whisper.

His laugh is soft and full of want and need. "I'll always help you Priss."

Smiling I lift up onto my tiptoes and kiss him, telling him without words that I'm his and that he's mine. When I open my eyes again and look at my sister, I feel a weight lift from inside of me and then settle again.

The will of a dead man ruined my life, and now somehow it's helping me put it back together again. Money is power and I lost a fortune, but maybe I found something much more valuable.

They say revenge is sweet, but the best form of revenge is to be better than those you seek justice from. Perhaps when this is all over I might be able to feel that way, but for now I'm looking forward to using all those lessons my parents taught me to reap a little of what they helped me sow.

My name is Carrigan Prudence Archibald and I'm not a good person. I've done things I'm not proud of, but I have a sister, and a boyfriend, and a life I'm ready to start embracing.

My parents spent most of my life ignoring me and my twin, then they spent four years using us. Now they think they can just walk away.

They're wrong.

The End
(As if I would be that cruel)
The Heir – Part Two coming soon

ABOUT THE AUTHOR

Gemma Weir is a half crazed stay at home mom to three kids, one man child and a hell hound. She has lived in the midlands, in the UK her whole life and has wanted to write a book since she was a child. Gemma has a ridiculously dirty mind and loves her book boyfriends to be big, tattooed alpha males. She's a reader first and foremost and she loves her romance to come with a happy ending and lots of sexy sex.

For updates on future releases check out my social media links.

ACKNOWLEDGMENTS

Let's be honest, so far 2020 has been a messed up old year. I expected to have released this entire series by now, but in March the world stopped spinning and so here I am in August and only just putting the finishing touches to this book.

I adore Carrigan and I really hope you do too. I've always been fascinated by the bad guys story and so I decided to give our evil twin a voice and it's been so fantastic to try and figure out what makes her tick.

What's also new about 2020 is that I was given the opportunity to sign with the fantastic Hudson Indie Ink. I'm so incredibly grateful to be working with such a fantastic team and I really hope this is the start of an incredibly successful future.

As always, I need to give a shout out to my bestie Sarah, she's been as impatiently waiting for this book as you guys have, but even when she's annoyed that I'm not writing, she's still there for me and a constant source of support. I literally wouldn't have made it through the last few months without her.

This world of the mega rich has let me embrace my inner

mean girl and I can't wait to write more about our kings and queens.

To my lovely and very patient readers, I've done it again and left you with a huge cliffy, but I'm just having far too much fun with this series to end it. Keep reading and I'll do my best not to having you screaming and throwing your kindles across the room with the next book.

Thank you so much to everyone who has helped me bring this book to life and happy reading.

ALSO BY GEMMA WEIR

The Archers Creek Series

Echo (Archer's Creek #1)

Daisy (Archer's Creek #2)

Blade (Archer's Creek #3)

Echo & Liv (Archer's Creek #3.5)

Park (Archer's Creek #4)

Smoke (Archer's Creek #5)

The Scions Series

Hidden (The Scions #1)

Found (The Scions #2)

Wings & Roots (The Scions #3)

The Kings & Queens of St Augustus Series

The Spare - Part One

(The Kings & Queens of St Augustus #1)

The Spare - Part Two

(The Kings & Queens of St Augustus #2)

The Heir - Part One

(The Kings & Queens of St Augustus #3)

OTHER WORKS FROM HUDSON INDIE INK

Paranormal Romance/Urban Fantasy

Stephanie Hudson

Sloane Murphy

Xen Randell

C.L. Monaghan

Sci-fi/Fantasy

Brandon Ellis

Devin Hanson

Crime/Action

Blake Hudson

Mike Gomes

Contemporary Romance

Eve L. Mitchell

Elodie Colt

Lightning Source UK Ltd.
Milton Keynes UK
UKHW012206021120
372671UK00001B/24

9 781913 904302